C.A. VARIAN

SEDUCED BY SASQUATCH

Book Cover by Leigh Cadiente

Art by ZONE ARTZ

Edited by Kate Seger

Chapter Header by Cuts and Prints Co.

Scene Break by microvone

Page Edge Design by Painted Wings Publishing, LLC

Contents

For the girlies who'll shoot a man on Saturday and fall for him on Tuesday,
For the girlies who like their romance tender, their monsters enormous, and their common sense optional, &
For the girlies who've always suspected Sasquatch would have better boyfriend potential than half the county,

This book is for you

CHAPTER 1

Squatchin' Birthday Blues

Olivia

I should have realized my brother's birthday was headed for disaster when he said, "Bring your boots, Liv—we're going squatchin'."

While most sisters expect dinner, cake, and maybe a cute selfie together, I was handed a flashlight, a rifle, and a promise that we'd "make history."

Around here, that phrase usually meant someone was going to end up muddy, drunk, or on the six o'clock news. But I would do anything for my big brother.

The weekend had actually started out normal enough.

Earlier that day

Friday morning dawned bright and hot. Heat shimmered off the gravel as I pulled into the range, and the smell of spent gunpowder clung to the air. A line of pickup trucks sat crooked along the fence, like a row of bad ideas.

The house where I grew up was twenty minutes back up the ridge, tucked behind a stand of pines where the road turned to dirt. Mama and Daddy left it to me when they passed away. My big brother, Gunner, already had a job in the city by then and said it made more sense for me to keep the place since I was the one taking care of it. He wasn't wrong; I had handled the bills, the dogs, and everything else since the day we buried them. He sent help when I needed it, but the land and the house were mine now. I guessed all those years of doing everything myself had carved a stubborn streak into me—one wide enough to argue with a man like T-Bone, a redneck Casanova we went to high school with who'd been chasing me ever since I was old enough to say no.

T-Bone leaned against the target frame by the firing line, looking like he thought the pose might win him a modeling contract. His sunglasses caught the glare, and that grin of his stretched too far to be sincere. He was one of those guys who believed he was more than he really was—God's gift and all that. I glanced toward the driveway, wondering how long it'd take for Gunner to show. He was supposed to meet me at the range later, but I wouldn't have minded him getting here early.

"Alright, Liv," he said, his Southern drawl dragging out the first word. "You just slide in right here, and I'll get behind you."

I looked at him, the thought making my skin crawl. "No."

He blinked, caught off guard. "What?"

"I said no. I can stand on my own."

He laughed, but it came out a little high. "Just makin' sure you got the right stance."

"I've got the right stance," I replied, setting my feet. "I Googled it."

Leaning his rifle against the wooden post, he huffed. "You can't learn shooting off the internet."

"You can learn anything off the internet," I said, cocking my rifle. "I fixed my dryer last week, learned how to can green beans, and even figured out how to tell a man to back off. Want me to demonstrate that one?"

He held up both hands, grinning wider, but his eyes dropped down my shirt like he couldn't help himself. I tightened my grip on the gun.

"I live alone," I said. "I stay feisty."

The first shot kicked hard against my shoulder, but the bullet hit dead center on the target. The sharp smell of gunpowder hit the back of my throat, and satisfaction rolled through me.

T-Bone let out a low whistle. "Look at you. Should've known a woman with legs like that would have aim."

Dropping my weapon, I rolled my eyes. "Why would those two things be related?"

He grinned. "Good balance."

"Uh-huh," I said. "You'd better back up before I test that balance again."

When he laughed, it was too loud and too fake. "I could take you out hunting—teach you to track. We could camp and spend time together in the dark."

He really couldn't fathom that a woman wouldn't appreciate his advances. "That's about the creepiest thing a man has said to me before noon."

He opened his mouth to argue, but a deep chuckle came from behind us. It was Gunner. Although my brother worked in the city, he had taken a long weekend off and planned to meet me at the range.

Gunner walked up with that half-smile of his, the one that always looked part proud and part sorry. He stood taller than most men and was broader across the shoulders, his beard catching the sunlight in streaks of brown and copper. Gunner never tried to look good, but it happened anyway. He had Daddy's build and Mama's eyes, both of which made people trust him more than they should.

"Are you all fighting or flirting?" he asked, his voice warm with amusement. He knew how much T-Bone riled me up, but they'd been friends since high school.

"Fighting," I said flatly.

"Mostly flirting," T-Bone added at the same time.

Gunner shook his head. "You'd better quit hitting on my sister, man. She's liable to feed you to a bear."

"She'd rather I was the one doing the eating," T-Bone said, waggling his eyebrows before firing another round downrange and missing so wide the target didn't even flinch—it was probably offended he'd aimed at it at all.

I didn't bother answering. Instead, I gave him a look that would make a crow drop dead mid-flight.

To my relief, he finally wandered off to bother somebody else.

Stepping up beside me, Gunner bumped my shoulder. "You're shooting well."

"Thank you. I'm shooting better than him."

He grinned. "That's my girl."

The pride in his voice caught me off guard. He'd taught me to throw rocks, ride bikes, and fix flat tires, and somehow, I still wanted his approval. Funny how that sticks, even at nearly thirty.

We fired a few more rounds together. The echo rolled across the ridge until it faded into the hum of cicadas. Brass casings littered the gravel, glinting in the sun. When the smell of powder finally thinned, Gunner leaned on the partition beside me, arms crossed, his grin lazy.

"Have you ever thought about coming out with us sometime?" he asked.

"Out where?"

"Up Hollow Ridge. The team is doing a big overnight trip this weekend. I want you to come."

I lifted my earmuffs and gave him a look. "You mean your Sasquatch club?"

He straightened, feigning offense. "My research team."

Huffing, I shook my head. "Research team? You're just four rednecks screaming at trees."

He laughed, completely unbothered. "We're serious this time. We've got motion sensors, night vision, bait traps—the whole operation."

"That sounds like a complete waste of time."

"It's my birthday," he said, flashing that smile again.

I groaned. "You're pulling the birthday card already?"

"Only one I've got."

His smile widened. Gunner always had a way of looking at people, as if he believed every wild idea might just work out if he pushed hard enough. I'd seen that look since we were kids, usually right before he broke something, and I had to fix it.

"Please, Liv," he said. "Come see for yourself. Just one night."

He nudged my elbow. "What, you scared you'll embarrass yourself in front of a bunch of dudes?"

I sighed. "Sometimes I think you only invite me to make fun of me."

"That's not true." He lifted his hand to his chin, pretending to think about it. "Maybe a little true."

I tried not to smile, but it slipped out anyway. "Fine. I'll think about it. But if T-Bone's there, I'm carrying my gun loaded."

"Fair enough."

Seeming satisfied with my answer, he clapped my shoulder, the gesture rough but affectionate. "You'll have fun, you'll see."

"I'll probably get eaten by mosquitoes."

"That too."

The shooting range emptied out one shooter at a time. Dust lifted in soft spirals across the gravel, and the smell of burnt powder lingered in the warm air. For a while, I just stood there, listening to the quiet return. Gunner's truck engine rumbled to life in the distance, gradually fading as he drove away down the hill.

I told myself it was just one night, that I was going for his sake, not mine. But deep down, beneath the sarcasm and sense, something restless stirred. Maybe it was curiosity. Either way, I already knew I'd go. And maybe—though I wouldn't admit it out loud—I wanted to see if there really was something out there that folks weren't supposed to see.

By the time I got home, the sun had dropped behind the ridge, and the sky had already begun to bruise from gold to blue. The porch boards groaned tiredly beneath my boots as I climbed the steps and set my gun on the table next to a chipped coffee cup filled with old paintbrushes.

Boone and June Bug bounded toward me, tails wagging as if I had been gone a week instead of half a day. Boone's deep bark rattled the porch rail while June Bug danced circles around my boots, nails clicking against the wood.

"Hey, y'all," I said, crouching down to scratch their ears. "No bears today—just T-Bone, which is worse."

After hanging up my jacket, I kicked off my boots and poured sweet tea over ice. The glass sweated in my palm while the frogs began their evening chorus beyond the porch.

Peace always came like that here—quiet, steady, and undeserved. This house had enough silence to hear yourself think, if you wanted to. I usually didn't. Thinking only raised questions I didn't care to answer: why I was still here when I could have left like Gunner did, why the mountains felt more like home than any place beyond them, and why I kept pretending that wasn't true.

Out on the porch, the swing waited as it always did. I carried my tea outside and eased down onto it, the chains creaking softly as I rocked. Fireflies blinked across the yard, small sparks floating through the thick dusk. Beyond the fence, mist gathered between the trees until the whole world turned to shadow.

The buzz of my phone against the armrest broke the stillness. It was Gunner.

"Gunner: You still thinking about it?"

"What?" I replied.

"Don't play dumb. Hollow Ridge. We're heading up tomorrow."

"I'm pretty sure I said I'd think about it."

"You owe me. Birthday clause."

A smile crept in before I could stop it. "You're impossible," I typed back.

Headlights appeared on the dirt road less than a minute later, bouncing over the ruts. So much for texting. I set my glass aside and braced myself for the impending storm.

The truck engine hadn't even quieted when my brother jumped out, arms full of papers, maps, and a cardboard container that smelled unmistakably like fried chicken. "You eat yet?" he called.

"I was fixing to."

"Good, because I brought supper." He stomped up the steps, spreading his maps across the porch table as if we were planning an invasion. "Look at this. Mason found a site right off the Appalachian

Trail—mile marker twenty-two. Multiple sightings. Even some hair samples."

"Hair samples?" I repeated, leaning over his chaotic spread. "Gunner, that looks like Google Maps."

"Maybe, but still—look at the map."

"I don't want to look at the map. I want to eat my chicken."

"Eat and look," he insisted, shoving the container toward me.

The smell hit first—grease, pepper, home. I sighed, took a leg, and said, "Why can't your birthday involve something normal? Bowling, maybe. A party."

"Because Sasquatch doesn't hang out at the bowling alley." He spoke around a mouthful of chicken. "This'll be fun. Mason's got a drone. We'll have eyes in the sky."

"That's what every woman wants on a Saturday night," I said. "Drones and bug bites."

He ignored my jab, tracing a finger along the paper. "We'll camp at the base of the ridge, set trail cams, and try a few calls. You don't even have to believe—just come keep me company."

I leaned back in the swing, which creaked under my weight. "You really think there's something out there?"

"I think there are a lot of things out there." His voice dropped to a soft, almost reverent tone. "You'd be surprised at what the woods hide."

That quiet note of wonder often caught me off guard. He'd slip it between all the nonsense and make it harder for me to dismiss him.

The porch light illuminated the tired lines around his eyes when he looked up. Gunner had aged in ways that weren't immediately apparent—still broad-shouldered, still boyish when he grinned, but worn around the edges. He worked too hard chasing dreams that didn't pay, and I figured I could give him one night to chase another.

"Fine," I finally said. "I'll go. But I'm not eating bugs, I'm not using leaves for toilet paper, and T-Bone better not try anything."

The grin that split his beard was pure triumph. "Deal."

The maps disappeared into a folder, and he started humming the theme from *The X-Files* while packing up. I watched him go, shaking my head but smiling anyway.

When his taillights vanished down the dirt road, the quiet settled back around me like a blanket. Frogs sang, and the wind stirred the leaves.

Leaning against the porch rail, I sipped what was left of my tea. An owl called once from the woods, the sound spookier than it should have been. Or at least, I believed it was an owl. Still, my gaze lingered on the tree line where the shadows thickened.

For a moment, the air felt too still. Something heavy shifted through the brush, cracking twigs underfoot. Gunner was getting to me—I wasn't usually the type to spook at night sounds.

It stopped right before I could decide whether I'd imagined it. Forcing my fears from my mind, I went inside and locked the door, telling myself it was nothing.

CHAPTER 2

When Rednecks Attack (the Forest)

Olivia

The following evening settled in with that heavy stillness that always signals rain. Clouds hung low over the ridge, and the air felt thick against my skin, like wet flannel. I kept checking the time, even though I knew Gunner would be late. Punctuality was not his strong suit.

Gear covered the kitchen table—boots, jacket, thermos, bug spray, an extra flashlight, and a packet of jerky I already regretted sharing. The gun sat last, cleaned and loaded. My eyes kept sliding back to it, like it was trying to talk me out of this whole mess.

A low rumble echoed up the mountain road, headlights bouncing between the trees. Then the SUV appeared: camouflage paint, mud-splattered and proud, with spotlights bolted to the roof and "Sasquatch Research Team" emblazoned in white letters on the side. It was a vehicle built by men with too much enthusiasm and nowhere near enough sense.

I sighed. "Lord, give me strength."

The truck barely came to a stop before Gunner jumped out, arms wide. "You ready, sis?"

"You're lucky I love you," I replied, taking in the red clay caked along the tires. Gunner's optimism was infectious, but his lack of concern for comfort was not. "That thing looks like it rides worse than a rodeo bull, and I already know I'm going to be itchy tomorrow."

He laughed, scooping me up as if I still weighed what I did in middle school. "You'll be glad you came once we get going!"

"Uh-huh." I fought the urge to roll my eyes as he set me down. "Where's this supposed to be again?"

"Southwest of Bryson City. Near the old trailhead."

"That's an hour away."

"Hour and ten," he said, sounding proud as if that made it even better.

Pulling my hood over my hair, I muttered, "You know, normal people celebrate birthdays with cake. There's still time."

"Sasquatch don't eat cake," he said. "Come on, you're going to love it."

"Doubt it," I said under my breath, but I followed him anyway, gravel crunching beneath my boots.

Halfway to the truck, I called, "Who's driving?"

The driver's door swung open before he could answer. A familiar drawl accompanied the red blink of a video camera. "Evening, Liv."

T-Bone. I didn't bother hiding my eye roll. Of course, it was him.

He grinned from the driver's seat. "Smile for the camera! History's about to be made."

"Yeah," I said, deadpan. "Probably historically bad decisions."

Oblivious, he chuckled while I muttered under my breath and hoisted my bag over my shoulder. For Gunner's sake, I forced a polite smile. "Hey, T-Bone."

"Didn't think you'd actually come," he said, tilting the camera. "Guess you couldn't resist me."

"Or maybe I lost a bet."

His laugh was obnoxious, and Gunner's wince said plenty. For half a heartbeat, I almost felt sorry for my brother—almost—but then I remembered this circus was his idea, and I was just a volunteer clown.

Voices spilled from the open doors, mingling with the scents of body spray and engine grease. Mason and Riggs were crammed in the back seat, arguing over some gadget that looked like it had been stolen from a sci-fi set.

"Hey, Olivia!" Riggs called, patting the seat beside him. He was married, so it was safe territory. I climbed in. "Didn't think we'd get you out here."

"Neither did I," I replied, waving to Mason. "How did your wife let you out on a Saturday night?"

"She's probably watching Hallmark with her sister right now. I'm doing her a favor."

"Good man." After buckling in, I added, "I would have opted for mint-chocolate-chip ice cream and Netflix, but here we are."

Gunner slid into the passenger seat just as T-Bone threw the SUV into drive. The engine groaned, rattling us like bees in a hive.

Trees crowded the narrow road, their branches skimming the doors as fog thickened around us. The smell of rain mixed with exhaust as we started down the hill. Headlights sliced through the fog, creating thin tunnels of light. Somewhere behind us, thunder rumbled—a deep sound that made the mountains feel alive.

I pressed my forehead against the window, watching the glow of my porch fade into the fog. "Happy birthday, Gunner," I said softly.

He grinned, completely unaware. "Best one yet."

I wasn't so sure.

The ride out stretched longer than a church service on Easter Sunday, full of noise that rattled my bones. From the driver's seat, T-Bone blasted the radio until the speakers whined, heavy metal riffs clashing with the clatter of gear in the back. Beside him, Gunner drummed on the dashboard, proud of his off-beat rhythm.

Behind me, Mason wrestled with a laptop connection while Riggs muttered about claustrophobia and coolers. I leaned my head against the cold window and watched the trees blur past in long, dark strokes.

As we climbed, the pines thinned into steep slopes, the shadows deepened, and lightning cracked across the horizon—bright enough to wash the world bone-pale before darkness swallowed it again.

"Prime sighting territory right here!" T-Bone hollered, grinning like a man who'd just actually discovered Sasquatch. "There was a whole cluster of reports last spring—huge prints, weird howls, the works!"

Without looking up, I replied, "Maybe all those 'reports' were just hikers who don't know a bear print from a boot print."

"Be nice," Gunner said with a grin. "If Bigfoot hears you talking like that, he'll haul you off first."

"His habitat smells like motor oil and a storm that's about to wash out the road," I shot back, which earned another laugh and a friendly slap on the shoulder. Half-joking or not, if we got stuck twenty miles from civilization, he wouldn't be getting any presents.

Conversation bounced around the cab until a pothole sent us airborne. Tires slammed down so hard my teeth clicked. Mud sprayed the windows, and the truck fishtailed before regaining its grip.

"Adds to the adventure," Gunner said.

"Adds to my chiropractor bill," I retorted.

Rain hammered on the roof, drowning our words in a low hum. Between bursts of lightning, glimpses of the forest flashed—slick trunks, silver moss, and the occasional glint of eyes watching from the dark. The longer we drove, the more I questioned my decision to join them.

Navigation turned into a group project. Mason swore the turnoff was still ahead; Riggs blamed magnetic interference with the GPS; Gunner unfolded a paper map that looked older than sin.

"You sure you boys even know where we're going?" I asked.

"Left at the fork," Gunner replied.

The view through the windshield made me laugh under my breath. "That's not a fork, Gunner. That's a ditch."

"Looks like a fork to me," he insisted.

I shook my head and reached for the 'oh shit' handle above the door. "Looks like death."

T-Bone turned left anyway. The SUV lurched, groaned, and then climbed steadily again, splashing mud that drenched the doors. Everyone whooped as if we had won a race none of us meant to enter.

We climbed higher into the mountains, the road narrowing until branches scraped both sides like long fingers. Rain thickened again, drumming a harder rhythm overhead. Our headlights pierced the fog, illuminating ghostly white swirls that vanished as quickly as they appeared.

Eventually, the noise softened to the engine's low growl. My mind drifted with it, half-listening and half-lost in the dark between the trees. Living out here, I had always wondered what truly watched from those woods. Bears, sure. Coyotes, definitely. But sometimes—when the world went still enough—it felt like something else breathed along with it. Something older.

I shook the thought off. That kind of nonsense belonged to bored teenagers and campfire stories.

Gunner's sudden whoop shattered my train of thought. "There it is! The old trailhead!"

T-Bone yanked the wheel, causing the SUV to fishtail again, and we skidded into a wide clearing surrounded by towering pines. When the engine died, silence rushed in and pressed at the edges of the clearing.

"Made it," I said, unclipping my seat belt. "Can't feel my spine, but we made it."

"Perfect spot," Mason replied, stretching. "Remote, flat ground, good sightlines."

Riggs popped open the cooler. "And I brought jerky."

"Small blessings," I murmured as I stepped into the mud, grateful I wouldn't have to share mine. Mist swirled around my boots in low, shifting coils. "So we're really camping here all night?"

"Sure are," Gunner answered, already shining his flashlight toward the trees. "Off the trail, though. You're about to see how professional this operation is."

My boots sank deeper into the muck, and the air turned heavier and sharper, carrying that moss and wet earth scent that always follows a storm. The trees closed around the clearing, their limbs tangled tightly enough to hide the sky.

Professional, huh.

Gunner popped his door open again. "Alright. Let's haul the gear to the fire ring. We'll set up base over that way."

"That way" turned out to be across a patch of ground the storm had turned into a mud pit.

I grabbed the first crate—heavier than it had any right to be—and followed him into the trees. The ground sloped just enough to make every step an argument. Roots crisscrossed under the muck, slick enough to yank my footing out from under me.

"Remind me again," I muttered, shifting the weight against my hip, "why we couldn't camp six feet from the truck like normal people?"

"Because then the footage looks staged," Gunner called over his shoulder. "We need natural terrain."

"The terrain is winning."

He snorted but didn't slow down.

We wove between the pines, all of us carrying something—tripods, crates, folding chairs, a cooler Riggs insisted on dragging instead of lifting. The path wasn't long, but the ground fought us every inch, sucking at our boots and splashing cold mud up our shins.

"Almost there," Mason said, though he'd said that twice already.

A branch snapped under T-Bone's foot, and he cursed as the cooler handle slipped from his grip. "Son of a—Riggs, you packed rocks in here?"

"High-protein snacks," Riggs answered. "Jerky doesn't weigh that much."

"Then something in here wants me dead."

Their bickering echoed through the fog. I adjusted my grip on the crate again, feeling the burn in my forearms. My shoulders tightened, my legs already protesting the uneven ground.

A gust of air pushed through the trees, carrying that cold, wet earth smell storms always leave behind. TThe forest around us held a weight the storm hadn't shaken off.

"Let's pick it up," Gunner said. "Storm's clearing fast."

By the time we reached the clearing he'd chosen—flat enough for tents, sheltered by pines—I dropped the crate onto the damp ground and rolled my shoulders. My thighs burned from the short haul, and mud climbed halfway up my jeans.

"That," I said, catching my breath, "was not a stroll."

"Told you it wasn't far," Gunner replied.

"Far isn't the issue," I grumbled. "The issue is gravity."

He grinned, completely unaffected, and motioned for the next haul.

We made several more trips before everything finally reached the clearing.

By the time the truck doors slammed, the woods had already swallowed the moonlight. Flashlights blinked on, their beams carving bright cones through the fog as everyone started talking at once.

Crates thudded into the mud as Gunner directed traffic as if he were setting up for a county fair instead of a scientific expedition. Mason crouched beside a tree, fiddling with wires and muttering about "voltage consistency." Riggs struggled with a tent that the wind seemed determined to steal.

Across the clearing, T-Bone filmed the chaos, narrating in his best documentary voice. "Here we have the elusive Sasquatch Research Team in its natural habitat, attempting to attract the creature with—wait for it—rotisserie chicken."

He swung the camera toward me. "Tell the folks at home what you think of the operation, Liv."

"Smells like regret and body odor," I replied.

He laughed and continued filming. Raindrops still hung in the air, and his light turned them into falling sparks—beautiful, if you ignored the man holding the camera.

Gunner strode past with an armload of motion sensors. "These go on the trees every twenty yards. Riggs, help Mason with the laptop. T-Bone, stop playing Spielberg and make yourself useful."

"Useful," T-Bone echoed. "Like... spiritually?"

Then Gunner's deadpan reply lands perfectly:

"Physically," Gunner responded without missing a beat.

The scene unfolded like slapstick theater. Tripods clanked, cords tangled, and every few minutes, someone yelped as a branch snapped back in their face. From my folding chair beside the fire pit, I sipped coffee from my thermos and thought that this whole production would have been a lot easier from my couch.

Still, I had to give my brother credit—he was in his element. Focus lit up his face, rain beading in his beard as he moved from one task to another. Every now and then, he'd glance my way and grin, that same proud-kid expression he'd worn at ten when he caught a frog, thinking it was proof of genius. Somehow, that grin still cracked my irritation in half.

After a few false starts, the fire finally came together. Sparks hissed into the damp air, and the smell of smoke mingled with wet leaves and chicken—an aroma sure to attract every raccoon in a five-mile radius. Steam rose from our jackets as we huddled close to the fire.

"Now we wait," Gunner said, wonder in his tone.

"Wait for what?" I asked.

"For signs—knocks, calls, eyeshine, anything un-usual."

My brow furrowed. "I'm surrounded by grown men, tripwires, and poultry. Everything about this is unusual."

Easy laughter circled the fire. Conversation flowed between jokes and tall tales, mostly past "almost sightings." Mason explained how motion sensors worked until I stopped pretending to understand. Riggs attempted a Sasquatch call he'd learned online; it sounded like a dying goose and sent T-Bone into hysterics.

Hours slipped by, and the rain faded to mist, and the forest glistened under the firelight. Crickets began to chirp again. Somewhere in the distance, a coyote howled. Beyond the ring of light, tall black trees stood, each one pretending to be something else.

I propped my boots on a cooler and leaned back in my chair. My body ached from the hike, and my eyes stung from the smoke, but a quiet eased through me anyway, the kind that shows up right before trouble.

"Hey, Liv," Riggs mumbled, half-asleep beside the fire. "Do you think he's out there watching us?"

I gazed into the darkness where our lights didn't reach. "If he is, he's probably embarrassed for us."

That earned a chuckle from the few still awake. One by one, voices faded until only the crackle of the fire and the whisper of the wind through the pine needles remained.

Somewhere in that quiet, a branch snapped.

Not close—just far enough to raise the small hairs on my neck.

I waited and listened, convincing myself it was nothing. Probably just a deer.

Still, my eyes lingered on the tree line longer than they should have. Eventually, I crawled into the tent, telling myself tomorrow we'd pack up, go home, and laugh about the night when nothing happened.

CHAPTER 3

The Night Sasquatch Flirted First

Olivia

It couldn't have been more than an hour since I'd crawled into the tent, but sleep kept slipping through my fingers. Heat clung to the tent walls, thick enough to make the air feel cramped. Every shift of the brush outside pulled me toward waking. By two in the morning, the woods had settled into a silence so complete it pressed against the edges of camp, broken only by the low crackle of the fire under the heavy, wet air.

Riggs had slumped in his chair, his hat tilted over his face; Mason's eyes were half-closed behind the glow of the laptop screen. Gunner was still pacing, his flashlight swinging like he was on patrol. And T-Bone—well, T-Bone sat on the tailgate "guarding the bait," which meant gnawing chicken bones and narrating his own heroism into the camera.

I was about one yawn away from heading back to the truck when nature called.

Grabbing my flashlight and strapping my rifle over my back—because, as Daddy always said, "you don't walk into dark woods with just good intentions"—I started toward the trees. "I'm going behind a bush!" I hollered.

T-Bone perked up like a hound dog. "You sure you don't need backup?"

"Boy, if I need backup to pee, I'm going home," I replied.

That earned a few laughs. Even Gunner cracked a grin. "Stay where I can hear you," he called. "Holler if it's a bear."

"It's gonna be y'all that get eaten," I muttered, stepping through the damp undergrowth.

The forest swallowed me fast. Just thirty yards out, and the fire was no more than a dull orange glow through the trees. Rainwater dripped slowly from the pines, each drop loud in the hush. The air smelled of sap and earth that hadn't been touched in years.

Finding a good patch of ferns, I took care of business and stood, stretching the ache from my legs. I was thinking about my warm bed and regretting my life choices when the sound came.

It wasn't the usual forest sounds. Something big shifted in the brush just beyond the beam of my light, and I went still.

Then came the breathing—slow and heavy enough to raise every hair on my arms.

My first thought was bear. My second thought was T-Bone, and that was somehow worse.

"Gunner?" I called, but my voice came out softer than I intended.

Silence.

I raised the flashlight, my hand trembling. The beam quivered across the ferns, up the slope, and then it caught on something-thick, matted fur, not sleek like a deer's, but dense and rain-soaked, with a deep copper sheen. My breath caught in my throat.

He stepped out before I could even move.

Mother Mary.

Standing upright like a man, he was as big as a barn door, with shoulders broad enough to make the trees look narrow. Water slicked down his fur, catching the faint gleam from my light. I should've run, should've screamed or fired my gun, but my boots seemed rooted to the ground as if the forest itself had decided I was part of it now.

Calm as anything, he didn't charge or growl. He just stood there, head tilted the way a curious dog might when trying to make sense of a noise.

But his eyes were the thing that held me the hardest. Golden-brown, bright even in the darkness, too intelligent to belong to a mere beast. They caught the light and held it, steady and almost soft, as if trying to communicate something.

Something in me forgot to be afraid.

"Hey," I whispered, my voice shaking anyway. "Hey there, big fella."

The creature shifted his weight, one massive hand resting against a tree trunk. When he breathed, I heard the slow drag of air, and I took a breath of my own. He made a low sound then—somewhere between a hum and a sigh—and it vibrated in my ribs like thunder rolling across a valley.

For a while, we simply watched each other. Maybe only seconds, but it felt like an eternity.

Then he took a step closer, and the ground seemed to respond to his weight. My flashlight jittered, illuminating his face. He wasn't just hair and shadow, as the stories suggested. He had a broad nose, a strong jaw, and the features of a man hidden beneath wildness.

I stood there, stunned, as his hand rose slowly and cautiously, palm turned away. When his knuckles brushed my cheek, I flinched, though only slightly.

His hand was warm. The hair was unruly but clean, coarse against my skin. The scent that clung to him—wet spruce, musk, and rain-soaked earth—settled around us. Not exactly pleasant, but not unpleasant either. Just... *alive*.

Behind me, someone called my name—Gunner, maybe, or T-Bone—interrupting the moment.

He turned at the sound, back toward the deeper parts of the forest.

"Wait," I breathed. I took a step after him, but he was gone. The darkness swallowed him until nothing remained but trees, leaving me in a state of surreal skepticism.

A moment later, flashlights flared, blinding me.

"Liv!" Gunner's voice was loud and panicked. "Are you okay?"

I lowered my arm to shield my eyes from the glare. "Yeah. I think so. There was a—" My words trailed off as I lifted my hand toward the direction the creature had disappeared, still unsure if it had actually happened.

T-Bone barreled up beside my brother, his camera already rolling. "Tell me you got footage. Please tell me you filmed him."

"He was right there." Hand trembling, I pointed at the trees. "He was big. Tall. Brown fur. He walked right up to me."

"You saw him?" Gunner's voice wavered between disbelief and triumph.

"For real," I said. "He touched me."

T-Bone nearly tripped over his own boots, trying to shine his light where I pointed. "Are you serious? Like, touched-touched?"

"Not like that, idiot." My throat tightened as I touched my cheek. "He just... checked me out. I don't know why."

Gunner looked like he was about to burst with joy. "I knew it! I told you all!"

The others whooped and clapped him on the back, but I barely heard them. My focus remained on the dark gap between the trees where he had vanished.

He hadn't been angry—nor was he scared—just... *curious.*

And, Lord help me, beneath the rush of fear, a part of me wanted to see him again.

Morning crept in, gray and heavy, dragging the smell of wet earth with it. Somewhere above the clouds, the sun was trying to rise, but its light barely broke through the fog. Everything was waterlogged—the tents, the air, my bones.

The boys were already up, their voices bouncing around camp like pebbles in a tin can. They were all talking about last night as if we hadn't nearly peed ourselves over the experience. Mason crouched beside the fire pit, poking at the wet ashes with a stick. Riggs sat cross-legged, muttering about corrupted files and camera angles. Gunner couldn't stop grinning, and T-Bone, Lord help me, still had that stupid camera glued to his hand.

"Morning, sunshine," he said, sweeping the lens in my direction. "Tell America how it feels to meet the myth."

I rolled over in my sleeping bag and pulled the hood down over my face. "Feels like a sinus infection," I muttered.

Gunner chuckled, bouncing on his heels. "She saw him, y'all! She talked to him. This is history in the making!"

"He did most of the talking," I said, sitting up slowly. "If you can call humming talking."

Riggs leaned forward, his eyes wide. "You touched him?"

"He touched me," I corrected, rubbing my cheek. "Right here."

That set them off again—questions flying, voices overlapping, all of them arguing about what it meant. Mason swore it was a "non-aggressive curiosity display." T-Bone suggested that maybe I'd triggered his "mating instincts."

"Say that again," I said flatly, "and I'll demonstrate my own non-aggressive display with a punch in the throat."

He laughed as if it were the best joke he'd ever heard, zooming in close with that darn camera. "Just saying, he didn't touch anybody else."

"Maybe because nobody else wandered off to pee in his living room," I replied, standing up to stretch. The damp air bit through my clothes, and steam rose from the ground as the sun finally broke through the fog.

Gunner was already packing gear, still buzzing with excitement. "We're coming back. I'm telling you—we set up more cameras and better lights, and next time we'll get proof. This is just the beginning."

"Beginning of a headache," I said, but I didn't bother arguing. That hopeful grin of his was hard to stomp on.

We loaded the truck in near silence, all of us too tired to maintain the excitement. The forest around us looked washed clean, wet trunks gleaming black, mist twisting between the branches like smoke.

Before climbing in, I turned once more toward the ridge. It looked empty and calm, like the whole night had been a fever dream. But as the others slammed the truck doors, I thought I caught a movement between the trees. Just a shadow watching.

Then it was gone.

Probably just my imagination. Probably.

T-Bone twisted around from the driver's seat, catching my reflection in the rearview mirror. "You sure you're okay, Liv? You look like you've seen a ghost."

I fastened my seatbelt and stared at the fog curling off the ground. "I did," I said softly. "He just wasn't dead."

CHAPTER 4

Sunday Scaries, Sasquatch Edition

Olivia

By the time they dropped me off, the fog had lifted from the ridge, leaving the morning too bright and too normal for what I had just witnessed. Gravel crunched under the SUV's tires as it pulled away, while Boone and June Bug barked from the porch, their tails wagging as if they didn't know the world had tilted sideways overnight. A pair of doves pecked at the feeder, oblivious to the strangeness of the day.

I stood in the driveway long after the SUV disappeared down the hill. The mountains looked the same—green, breathing, and ancient—but they didn't feel the same. Something in me had changed, and even the air felt different. My hands shook at my sides, a tremor I couldn't quiet.

Hours had passed since I had left the campsite, yet the memory of those eyes and that almost-human stillness stuck with me. He had looked at me as if I were more than just a noise in his woods. That thought lodged deep within me, colder than fear.

"Get a grip," I muttered, reaching for my bag. "You're losing it."

Boone bounded down the steps, his nails clattering on the boards, while June Bug yipped from behind him. They swarmed my legs as I approached the porch, their wet noses against my hands. Their familiar weight steadied me in a way that words couldn't.

"I'm fine," I told them, even though neither seemed convinced. Boone huffed, and June Bug's tail beat the air like a metronome.

Inside, the house smelled the same as when I left. Lemon cleaner and coffee grounds, familiar scents that usually soothed me. Today, those same smells tightened the walls around me, turning the quiet sharp. I dropped my things by the door and headed straight for the shower.

Steam filled the bathroom, fogging the mirror, but no amount of heat could chase away the chill in my chest. Hot water and strong coffee were supposed to burn off nerves, but they didn't. The unease kept building with every minute, until even the sound of the clock on the wall felt sharp.

I tried to immerse myself in work. The glow of my laptop screen stared back at me like an accusation. "Create something," it seemed to say, but the cursor blinked like a heartbeat, and I couldn't make my mind cooperate. I designed websites for small-town clients—feed stores, antique shops, the occasional church fundraiser—people who still believed the Internet was a living thing that needed taming. That usually centered me and gave me a sense of purpose. But not today.

Today, my own breathing distracted me. My thoughts kept ricocheting around.

I told myself not to look out the window, but I did anyway.

The trees stood still, the yard was empty, and the porch swing rocked slowly in the wind. Nothing seemed out of place, yet the quiet felt wrong, stretched too thin to be natural.

Closing the laptop, I grabbed my mug and stepped onto the porch. Boone followed closely at my heel, while June Bug slipped past and onto the steps, her ears pricked forward. A coming-rain smell hung in the air—sweet, with a metallic edge. Thunder rumbled far off, its voice low, echoing the sound of something awakening beneath the hills.

"Do y'all smell anything?" I asked, though my voice came out thinner than I intended.

Before I saw anything unusual, Boone's growl began deep in his throat, rumbling up through the porch boards. June Bug's tail stiffened. Both dogs froze in that way dogs do when their instincts take over.

A branch cracked beyond the fence, a sharp sound that felt too heavy to be made by a squirrel.

My heart pounded hard. "Could be a deer," I said, mostly to myself. The words tasted like a lie, a feeble attempt to calm the rising fear within me.

The wind shifted, bringing a scent that didn't belong—musk, earth rich with rain, and something else beneath it, something alive. A smell that made my body still itself without asking me.

My hand found the doorknob. "Not doing this," I whispered, my voice trembling with dread. "Nope. Not today."

Before I could stop them, the dogs lunged, racing down the steps and barking as if they had found the devil himself. "Boone! June Bug!" My voice barely carried over their noise.

Movement flickered between the pines, something broad, brown, and moving with a purpose. Not the awkward rush of a deer or the skittish dart of a coyote. It moved slowly, as if it were watching.

"Lord, have mercy," I breathed.

The shape vanished as quickly as it had appeared.

Boone barked until his throat went hoarse, and June Bug circled, growling low. I stood frozen, coffee gone cold in my hand, trying to convince myself it was a trick of the light. But deep down, I knew the truth sat solid and heavy.

It was *him*.

He had followed me home.

Heart thrashing against my ribcage, I called the dogs inside, shut the door, and leaned against it until the wood stopped shaking under my palms. The house felt smaller than before, and the air was too thin to breathe.

Still, I couldn't stop pacing from window to window, each creak of the floor reminding me that something was waiting outside. The porch light spilled a yellow glow across the yard, cutting a narrow line into the trees.

"Fine," I muttered. "If he's out there, he's going to see me looking like hell, and maybe that will scare him off."

The dogs followed me with their eyes but didn't bark. They knew the rhythm of my restlessness. I poured another cup of coffee, more for something to do than to drink, and stared out through the rain-blurred glass.

Nothing moved. Just the steady hiss of drizzle and the flicker of the porch light.

Then the shadows shifted. A darker shape slid behind the glow—too solid to be a trick, too fluid to be human.

Boone's growl rolled out first, deep and warning. June Bug joined him with a higher bark that snapped through my nerves. My stomach tightened, breath catching halfway down my throat. A cold tremor ran from my fingertips to my elbow, the coffee sloshing in my hand. I set the cup down before I dropped it.

"It's just a bear," I whispered. The words came thin and cracked. "A big, wet, hungry bear."

I grabbed the gun because my hands needed something to hold. Sweat made my grip slip once, and my pulse stumbled hard enough to shake my knees.

Rain hit the steps in silver splashes when I opened the door. The familiar smell of wet grass rolled over me.

And beneath it—breathing.

Not loud. Not close. Just steady enough to shove my pulse into a sprint.

Lightning tore across the sky.

For a heartbeat, the yard flashed bright.

And he stood there.

Massive. Still. Rain tracking down fur the color of copper bark. The same impossible shoulders. The same gold-brown eyes staring straight at me — eyes that followed me with too much understanding and none of the distance a wild animal should have.

My whole body locked. Heat rushed up my throat, even as a cold shock hit my chest. My breath broke into short bursts. My hands shook so violently that I almost lost the gun.

I didn't think. I didn't aim. Instinct fired before I could stop it.

The thunder came first. The recoil slammed into my shoulder. The world cracked open around me.

The bullet hit him. His body jolted, and a guttural cry tore from his chest. For an instant, hurt flashed through those bright eyes. Then he turned, stumbling as he disappeared into the trees.

The echo of the shot rolled down the ridge and back again, long after he was gone.

Rain poured onto the porch, cool against my bare feet. "Dear God," I whispered. "What did I do?"

The guilt hit harder than I expected, and I locked the door and slid down against it, the gun still heavy in my hand and my heart thundering against my ribs. He had come to me again—not to harm me—and I had shot him.

The storm never really stopped as I stood there, mind whirling. Rain pattered softly on the roof, steady and soft, while the house sat still around me. Boone and June Bug lay curled beside the door, their ears twitching whenever the wind shifted. I had long since set the gun aside, but my hands kept reaching for it anyway, fingers remembering the recoil.

Every time I closed my eyes, I saw him flinch—the way his shoulders bowed, the shock that wasn't anger but hurt. The moment replayed the second I closed my eyes.

"I didn't mean to," I whispered to no one. Boone lifted his head, whined once, then settled again.

I pushed to my feet before I could talk myself out of it. "You stay here," I told them, though my voice had gone soft. They didn't move, only watched as I pulled on my raincoat and shoved my feet into muddy boots.

When I stepped onto the porch, the storm breathed in. Rain cooled my face the moment I stepped outside, washing the warmth from my skin. The yard stretched quietly beneath the porch light—a narrow strip of yellow fading into the dark pines.

"Please don't be dead," I said into the rain. The words vanished before they reached the trees.

The flashlight beam cut through the mist, a trembling line of white that found small, dark stains in the grass. I crouched low. The drops had thinned with the rain but hadn't vanished yet. *Blood.*

My stomach turned. "Oh, Lord," I breathed. "What have I done?"

The trail led past the fence and down into the trees. I followed it, my heart hammering, each step sinking into mud that tried to pull me back. The forest muted everything except the rain—no crickets, no wind, only the steady drip through the leaves and the dull thud of my heartbeat.

The pine smell grew stronger the farther I went, laced with the iron tang of blood and wet earth. A flicker of motion ahead made me freeze, but it was just the light catching slick bark.

"Hey," I called softly, my voice shaking. "It's me. I'm not gonna hurt you."

No answer. Just the sound of rain easing into mist and the slow drip from the branches above.

I kept walking until the beam swept across a fallen log near the bottom of the hollow. He was there.

Slumped against the trunk, the Sasquatch had one arm braced to keep himself upright. Rain ran off his fur in thin silver streams, and blood darkened the shoulder where the bullet had hit him. His chest rose and fell in a shallow rhythm, but he was breathing. *Alive.*

Relief washed through me so fast I had to stop.

I stopped a few steps back, not daring to move closer. "I'm sorry," I said, my voice cracking. "I thought you were a threat. I didn't know."

He lifted his head slowly, his eyes meeting mine.

The flashlight trembled in my hand as I moved closer to him, every muscle in my body tight with guilt.

When I reached out to check his arm, he flinched once but then went still. His skin felt fever-hot beneath my fingers, radiating heat that shouldn't have been possible. The muscles under my hand were solid and human in their tension, but the texture of his fur—slicked down, coarse at the tips but soft underneath—felt wild, like everything outside had left its mark on him.

"You're bleeding too much," I whispered. "I've got to bandage this."

He made a low, rough sound deep in his chest, like exhaustion transformed into breath. His eyes flicked toward mine at the offer to bandage him—just a slight movement, but enough to make me pause.

"You understand me," I said quietly, realizing it wasn't a question.

Thunder rumbled across the valley, faint but ominous.

I glanced toward the dim glow of my porch light filtering through the trees. "You can't stay out here," I said. "You'll bleed out or get an infection. Come with me. I'll help you."

Although he didn't respond, when I stepped back, he tried to rise, still holding his arm. His breath hitched, and his hand pressed against the tree for balance. Slowly, painfully, he managed to stand.

"Easy now," I murmured. "Slow and steady."

He leaned against the trunk for a moment longer before taking a step. Even that small movement made the ground tremble beneath us. Still, I swallowed back my fear and lifted the flashlight, guiding our way home.

CHAPTER 5

How to Accidentally, on Purpose, Shoot a Legend

Olivia

Rain had faded to a thin drizzle by the time we reached the barn. My porch light glowed behind us through the fog, casting a muted halo I refused to look back at. If I did, I'd turn around and lock myself inside.

The hinges shrieked when I pulled the big sliding door open, a sound sharp enough to make him flinch. "Sorry," I whispered before I could stop myself. I wasn't sure how much he understood, but the way his eyes tracked my mouth told me he caught something.

Cool, damp air met us, carrying the scents of hay, old oil, and wood darkened by years of storms. The barn always held the smell of work already done, but tonight it felt different; the air felt tight enough to notice, even if I couldn't explain why. A distant rumble rolled through the hills. Water dripped steadily from the eaves, each drop marking the quiet.

Behind me, he paused in the doorway, broad shoulders tight under the frame. Lantern light traced the damp fur along his arms and outlined him in a soft, uneven glow.

"It's dry," I said quietly. "That's something, at least."

He made a low sound deep in his chest, not quite agreement and not quite warning. His eyes—deep gold catching every shift of light—moved across the space, from the stalls to the low rafters and finally to me. Caution lived there, but so did awareness. He wasn't turning away, and that felt like its own kind of answer.

I stepped farther inside, found an old quilt folded on a shelf, and spread it across a thick pile of hay. "Here," I said, patting the spot. "Sit down before you fall down."

For a moment, he didn't move. Then, he stepped forward, careful as if the floor might give way beneath him. Every movement had its own controlled weight, a balance of weight and restraint bound together. When he lowered himself onto the quilt, the old boards moaned in protest. I exhaled slowly.

"I'll be right back," I said, forcing my voice to steady. "Don't go anywhere."

Outside, the night air clung warm and damp against my skin. I ran for the house, my boots sinking into the soft earth, with Boone and June Bug barking at my heels. Inside, I grabbed the first-aid kit, a clean towel, bottled water, and a small bottle of ibuprofen from the cabinet. My hands weren't steady as I poured the water into another glass and slapped together a sandwich—ham, cheese, and mustard—simple and *human*.

"Lord above, don't let this be a mistake," I murmured, looking down at the pill bottle in my hand. "If this hurts him, I'll never forgive myself."

When I returned to the barn, he was still seated on the haystack, waiting for me to return like I'd asked him to do. I still wasn't sure how much he understood, but I wasn't sure I was ready to know those answers yet either.

"I brought some things," I said softly, setting everything down beside him. "Water, food, and medicine. It'll help with the pain."

His head lifted at the sound of my voice, my breath stilling when our eyes met. At that moment, the thought of anyone tracking him down and studying him like some science project turned my stomach.

"I need to clean your shoulder first," I continued after pulling myself out of my head. "Then you can eat."

He made no move to stop me when I leaned in close to him. The rain had rinsed most of the blood and dirt away, but the wound was deep and still trickled red beneath the lantern's glow. I dipped the towel again, pressing gently until the bleeding slowed. My focus stayed fixed on the motion—cloth to skin, breath to rhythm—until I realized how close I'd leaned in. The warmth coming off him wasn't just heat; it was presence. It filled the small space between us in a way I couldn't ignore, but somehow, I felt safe.

When my hand brushed lower, I couldn't help but notice how the fur thinned across his torso and hips, revealing the shape beneath. The shadows softened him, but not enough. The sight jolted through me before I could look away. I caught my breath, the heat climbing the back of my neck.

Focus, Olivia. You're tending a wound.

I forced my eyes back to his shoulder, where the blood welled along the edges of the gash. Some things didn't need clear light to be understood, and I had no business thinking about any of them just then.

"This'll sting," I warned quietly. "Don't hit me."

His breath rolled out in a low, vibrating sound that almost passed for a laugh.

The noise startled me, and I realized he recognized my tone—even if the words slipped past him.

Clenching my teeth, I poured the disinfectant over the wound and blew across the torn skin to blunt the sting. His whole body tensed, muscles shifting beneath the fur as a guttural noise tore from his chest. I flinched with him and murmured, "I know, I know it burns. Just hang on."

His golden gaze snapped up.

And this time, the truth landed hard: he wasn't reacting to tone—he was following the words.

Dragging my eyes away, I pressed a clean towel against the wound until the bleeding eased. His skin startled me—tough but smooth, something between hide and flesh. His pulse thudded steady beneath my fingers, deep in a way that felt anchored in him.

"You're lucky," I whispered. "It could've been worse. It just grazed you."

A low sound rose from his chest, something that might've meant agreement. Gradually, his breathing slowed, the tension in his frame loosening one careful breath at a time. The wound probably should have been stitched, but I did not have the nerve. I wasn't even sure human skin rules applied to him.

When the bleeding stopped, I tore a strip of gauze and wrapped it across his shoulder, tucking the edge to hold it in place. My fingers brushed his skin as I tied the bandage, and the heat of him lingered against my palms. It was impossible to ignore.

"Alright," I said softly, sitting back on my heels. "Now for the medicine."

He watched me without moving, the lamplight slipping across his face in bands of gold and shadow. The curiosity in his eyes wasn't human exactly. Still, it wasn't feral either—it was something that lived in the space between.

Pouring a few pills out of the bottle, I let them rest in my palm. "It's for pain," I explained. "You swallow them. It'll make you feel better."

He cocked his head slightly, listening to the sound of my voice. The soft rasp of his breath filled the quiet. I lifted one pill to my mouth, swallowed it, and opened my hand to show him. "See? Safe."

For a moment, nothing happened. Then he reached out, his hand massive and covered in fur, and took the pills from my palm with a gentleness I didn't expect.

Next, I passed him the glass of water. He sniffed it once, then drank, each swallow visible in the movement of his throat. The sound was ordinary, almost domestic, and that ordinariness undid me a little. Watching him like that—cautious but trusting—did something strange to my chest, as if my heart had shifted into unfamiliar territory.

"Good," I murmured. "That should help."

Outside, the storm had softened into stillness. The frogs had begun their tentative calls, the first few voices testing the quiet. I reached for the sandwich and held it out to him. "Here. Eat."

He studied it the way he studied everything—with patience that felt learned rather than instinctive. One cautious sniff, a low huff, then he took a small bite. The sight nearly pulled a laugh out of me: this enormous creature chewing carefully, as if trying to remember how food was supposed to work.

I took a bite of my own half, pretending it was normal. "Not bad, huh?"

A deep rumble moved through him, the sound vibrating in my ribs. It wasn't a growl, really. It was too content for that.

"I'll take that as a yes," I said, the corners of my mouth lifting despite myself.

When he finished eating, I handed him the last of the water. He drank again, slower this time, his gaze lifting to mine as if to make sure I approved. There was nothing animal in that look. Only a quiet and unsettling awareness.

The lantern light shifted when he leaned back, tracing the lines that crossed his chest. Long, pale scars ran beneath the fur like rivers under snow. Old wounds, healed over time, still refusing to fade. My breath caught. He wasn't wearing anything, but the moment didn't feel indecent. Maybe it was the way he held himself—unashamed, unconcerned with the boundaries that governed people. The fur covered most of him, but not enough to hide what he was.

Not a beast. Not a man. Something caught in between.

"You've been hurt before," I said quietly. "Not just tonight."

He blinked once, then the gold in his eyes dimmed, like a lantern turned low. The sound that followed wasn't a growl—it was softer, almost mournful.

I wanted to ask who had done it. What had happened? But the words stuck somewhere behind my teeth. Whatever he'd endured, he'd survived it. And tonight, I'd added another wound to the list.

The light flickered, and his face shifted with it—shadows slipping across the hollows beneath his eyes. His breathing had steadied, deep and even, but the sound carried through the barn, sharp enough that I felt my own heartbeat pick up. Guilt twisted my chest until I thought it might burst.

"You shouldn't exist," I whispered before I could stop myself.

"I didn't mean it like that," I said quickly. "I just—there's no one else like you."

The silence that followed was absolute. Even the rafters felt unnervingly still. Rain tapped once against the roof and stopped, leaving only the slow, living sound of him breathing.

"You need rest," I said finally, rising to my feet. "I'll check on you in the morning."

Although he didn't stand, his eyes followed me as I moved toward the door, his gaze catching the lantern light, too alive to belong to anything imagined.

Blowing out a shaky breath, I closed the door gently. The light inside shrank to a thin gold thread, glowing through the cracks until it disappeared.

Sleep wouldn't come. I lay beneath the quilt, staring at the ceiling beams while my mind refused to settle. Each small creak put me on edge; every tap of the branches against the roof sounded too much like footsteps. Boone and June Bug slept near the door, completely unfazed. They trusted the quiet. I didn't.

My thoughts kept drifting back to the barn, to the shape of him breathing in the dark, to the way those gold eyes followed me even after I pulled the trigger. I kept listening for something heavier than rain—anything that might tell me whether he'd moved or left or simply stayed where I'd last seen him.

But the guilt wasn't the part that kept me awake.

It was the question I hadn't let myself ask until now:

Why did he follow me home? What had he wanted when he stepped out of the trees? What made him walk straight toward my porch light as if he'd come straight to me on purpose?

The questions tightened my stomach more than the memory of the gunshot ever had.

"Lord, what am I supposed to do with this?" I whispered into the dark.

The house stayed quiet.

Rolling onto my side, I pulled the quilt tighter. The sense of him lingered. Not a smell, exactly. More a warmth, the echo of his pulse beneath my hands when I bound his shoulder. I'd washed twice, yet the feeling clung like static, impossible to shake.

Each time I closed my eyes, I saw the lantern light on his fur, the rise and fall of his chest, those gold eyes when I'd said he shouldn't exist. That look burned the deepest. He hadn't been angry; he'd looked wounded. As if he understood more than I'd meant to say.

It didn't make sense. None of it did. He was too human to be a legend, too wild to be a man. He bled and breathed and moved like both, carrying a gravity that felt older than either of them.

My hand found my chest, right where I'd felt his heartbeat through my palm. The warmth pulsed there still. Touching him hadn't felt wrong—just unfamiliar, like standing too close to a storm, waiting for whatever might break next.

"Get a grip," I muttered. "You're lying here mooning over Sasquatch."

The humor fell flat. What unsettled me most wasn't that I'd seen him—it was that I wanted to see him again.

Boone stirred once and sighed. June Bug's paw twitched. The night was so quiet the clock down the hall sounded louder than it should. I thought about getting up and checking the barn. But I knew myself too well. If I went out there, I wouldn't stop at the doorway. I'd want to see his eyes again—to hear that low hum that didn't quite sound human.

"He's out there sleeping like a log," I whispered, "and I'm in here losing my mind."

Darkness pressed close around me. Somewhere outside, an owl hooted, then went silent again.

For a moment, I thought I heard something else—not thunder, not wind, but a sound too deep to be either. It rose from the direction of the barn, low and even, like the heartbeat of the land itself. I held my breath. The hum came again, quiet but clear. Not a growl. Not a cry. Just a vibration that felt gentle somehow—like he was dreaming.

My throat tightened. I wanted to believe I'd imagined it, but I recognized that sound. It was the same one he'd made when I touched his shoulder. The sound that lived somewhere between pain and understanding.

I lay awake long after it faded, my hand pressed to my chest, feeling the echo move through me like warmth. By the time my eyes finally closed, dawn had begun to gather at the window, washing the room in a dim, colorless light.

The hum drifted with me into sleep, so quiet I almost believed I'd dreamed it.

CHAPTER 6

Coffee, Eggs, and Existential Crises

Olivia

The storm broke sometime before dawn, leaving the world washed and still. I could tell by the way the soft light slid through the curtains that it was already late morning—later than I usually slept.

For a long while, I stayed in bed, listening. The dogs slept heavily near the door, Boone on guard even in his dreams, while June Bug sprawled on her back without a care. I should have been able to rest too, but my thoughts kept wandering back to the barn—to the bandage, the steady rise of his chest, and the sound of that low hum fading into the night. My chest tightened whenever I thought about the stranger in the barn, his pain becoming my own.

Yesterday, guilt kept me awake. Today, it was curiosity that was pushing me toward the barn whether I was ready or not.

I tried to tell myself to wait until noon, just in case he was still resting, but impatience had always been my downfall. By the time the coffee pot hissed, I was already pulling on my boots.

"Stay," I told the dogs, my voice firm but gentle. "No barking, no running. You got it?"

Boone huffed like he understood, while June Bug wagged her tail anyway.

The yard sparkled under the thin sunlight, every blade of grass heavy with condensation. The air carried that washed-clean scent the mountains always held after a storm. It felt like the kind of morning that offered second chances. A few birds called from the ridge—warblers, maybe—and a doe grazed with her fawn near the tree line. *Second chances.*

When I reached the barn, I paused with my hand on the door, my heart beating too fast for what I kept telling myself wasn't a big deal.

The barn was quiet when I opened the door, lit by the gray, post-rain light filtering through the boards.

The Sasquatch sat where I'd left him, the quilt loose around his shoulders, his eyes lifted to the thin cracks in the wall where sunlight spilled through like thin streaks of gold cutting through the dim. The bandage still held, though a strip of gauze had shifted along the edge of his arm.

A low creak from the hinges made him glance over his shoulder. That single look froze me in place.

"Hey," I said softly. "Morning."

No answer came, but his gaze stayed on me as I crossed the threshold.

"Did you drink any water?" I asked, nodding toward the glass I'd refilled the night before. It sat half empty. "Guess so."

A slow tilt of his head met my voice, more curiosity than confusion, but he did not respond.

Stepping closer, I reached for his arm to check the bandage. The gauze was clean, with edges darkened only where the blood had dried. When my fingers brushed the edge, a faint tension rippled through his shoulders, but he didn't pull away.

"Still looks good," I murmured. "No fever, no bad color. You're a tough one."

His eyes never left my hands. The steady rhythm of his breath held a quiet focus I couldn't miss. He seemed to be measuring my intent more than my words. When I finally sat back, his attention drifted toward the worktable along the wall, landing on my daddy's old radio—the kind that never came in clear but always tried.

The sight of it held him still. A faint furrow drew between his brows before his gaze slid back to me.

"Sound," he said at last, his voice rough like gravel. The word dropped into the quiet with unexpected weight, like a pebble sinking into deep water.

I blinked, unsure I had heard him correctly. "Yeah," I managed. "It makes sound."

His lips formed another word, his voice cautious. "Song." The word emerged like a memory pulled from the back of his throat. After not hearing him speak for two days, this second word came as a surprise.

"You... you know music?" My voice barely found itself.

He didn't answer, but his expression shifted, understanding sparkling behind his eyes. He turned his gaze toward the window, where a shaft of light cut through the dust. He lifted his hand into it, palm open, and watched the light sifting across his skin. The gesture was so simple, so human, it ached to witness.

"You had people once, didn't you?" I said quietly. "You weren't always alone."

When his eyes met mine again, something moved through them—grief, soft and wordless, stirring like wind in tall grass.

My throat tightened. "You know music," I mur-mured, just to break the silence. "Maybe that's something we can work with."

The sound that followed wasn't quite a word or a sigh; just a low breath with meaning buried within it.

I rose to my feet, mostly to steady myself. "You stay put, alright? I'll bring breakfast. Maybe we can see if that old radio still plays a tune."

Outside, the fog had begun to lift from the ridge, sunlight threading through the trees in thin, bright lines. The morning felt delicate, as if it hadn't settled fully into itself yet.

I realized I was smiling.

Although I wasn't sure what counted as break-fast for a creature like my unexpected visitor—or victim—it felt wrong to bring nothing at all. So I prepared what I knew: two fried eggs, a heel of bread, and a couple of apples that were just one good day away from spoiling. I set a glass of water beside it all and carried the tray out before I could talk myself out of it.

By then, sunlight stretched across the yard in long bands. The air was already warming, still damp enough to taste the night before. Boone barked once from the porch, more curious than protective, and June Bug trailed behind me until I waved her off.

"Stay," I said. "You'd scare him worse than the gun did."

The hinges protested as I pushed the door open. He turned toward me again, just like before, but this time his shoulders didn't tense. His eyes flicked to the tray, then back to me, and something softened in his face. He wasn't used to being cared for.

"I didn't know what you'd eat," I said, setting the tray on the old workbench. "So I guessed."

He watched every motion as I arranged the food, nostrils flaring at the smell of the eggs. When I stepped back, he leaned forward, sniffed once, then carefully reached for the bread. He held it like it might crumble if he wasn't gentle.

"Go on," I said. "It's not poison."

He looked up at me before taking a bite. His teeth were blunt, more human than I expected, and the sound he made—a half sigh, half hum—almost made me laugh.

"Guess you eat what I eat," I said. "Glad we cleared that up."

While he ate, I fetched the little radio from the shelf. The dial stuck halfway between stations, as it always did. Still, after some patience and static, I found an old honky-tonk channel. A fiddle wove through the static like it remembered heartbreak from another lifetime.

He froze. His head tilted toward the sound, and his whole body went still. The bread hung forgotten in his hand.

"It's music," I said softly. "A song."

His eyes flicked to me. A quiet rumble slipped from his chest—almost thoughtful—before he echoed, "Song."

It wasn't clear. More breath than word.

I blinked hard, convinced I'd imagined it.

"You… said something?" My voice barely carried.

He didn't answer. His gaze drifted back toward the radio, toward the fiddle weaving through the static. The old man's voice followed, rough around the edges with talk of mountains and home.

Then, with the same careful focus he gave every new thing, he touched his chest and repeated it—clearer this time.

"Song."

My heart stumbled.

This wasn't mishearing.

This wasn't luck.

"You really can speak," I whispered, the truth landing with a weight that stole my breath.

A faint change touched his expression—not quite a smile, not quite sorrow—just a shift that made him look undeniably human. He held still, listening again, as if every note mattered.

The air between us felt different now, charged in a way I couldn't explain. Something was beginning, and I didn't know what to do with it.

After a while, he turned his gaze back to me. His mouth opened, hesitated, then he said, "You."

The sound came out soft and uncertain, the word itself surprising him as much as it did me.

"My name?" I asked. "Is that what you mean?"

When he nodded, my pulse jumped. "Yeah," I said quietly, pointing at my chest. "Liv. My name is Liv."

I swallowed. "And your name," I asked, motioning toward him. "What's your name?"

For a long moment, he only looked at me. The light from the doorway cut across his face, catching the strange gold in his eyes. I could hear the rasp of his breath, the creak of the floor under his weight. Then his lips parted, and he touched his chest again.

"Vek," he said.

The word was short, rough-edged, but it held something solid. Like the sound itself had roots.

"Vek," I echoed, and the name lingered in the air between us, heavier than it should've been. Saying it felt like opening a door I didn't know existed.

He watched my mouth as I spoke it again, softer this time. His eyes darkened with something that looked almost like relief.

The quiet pressed close around us, too intimate, too much. My pulse wouldn't settle. I needed a breath that didn't belong to the same moment. "I'll be right back," I murmured, finding my feet before my thoughts could.

I stepped toward the doorway, letting the cooler air hit me, the name still curling through my mind like a promise I wasn't ready to hold. Outside, the air cooled the heat still tangled in my chest. I stood there for a moment, trying to steady my thoughts.

For the first time since that night, I felt something I hadn't dared to feel before.

Hope.

Hope for what? I didn't even know.

But hope felt fragile in a way I didn't trust.—not after everything I'd seen. It pressed against my ribs, too new and too fragile to trust.

For the first time since this whole mess began, I didn't feel hunted. The woods didn't feel heavy or haunted; they just felt alive. And the visitor in my barn? He wasn't a beast anymore. He had a name... Vek.

Behind me, the barn door stood cracked open, the soft sound of the radio spilling out and mingling with the morning breeze. Through the gap, I could still see him sitting in that slant of light, a quilt draped across his shoulders, his head tilted toward the music as if it were the first thing that had made sense in years.

For a moment, I leaned against the porch post and took a slow breath, letting the weight of it all settle.

He'd spoken. Not just a sound, not a noise—but words. Our names.

And the way he'd looked at me afterward wasn't wild or strange or threatening. It was human—maybe more human than half the men I'd ever met. Definitely more human than T-Bone.

I rubbed the back of my neck, the truth settling heavy like the humidity. "Lord help me," I muttered. "I've lost my damn mind."

June Bug barked once from the porch, breaking my spiral, her tail swishing through the puddles. Boone followed her with a low chuff, both of them watching the barn as if they knew exactly what I was thinking.

"Don't look at me like that," I said. "I didn't plan this."

The wind moved through the pines, soft as laughter. Somewhere up the ridge, a truck engine groaned and faded—the world still turning, unaware that something impossible was breathing in my barn.

I pushed off the post and started back toward the house. "One step at a time, Liv," I told myself. "Feed him. Keep him hidden. Try not to lose your mind."

Halfway across the yard, I stopped. The air still held the echo of a storm, the kind that settled deep no matter how warm the air turned. Vek was in there with nothing but a quilt and a lantern, still damp from the rain. For all I knew, he had a home somewhere deep in the mountains, and I had him sleeping on an itchy bale of hay.

"Dammit," I muttered, guilt moving back in.

Returning inside the house, I grabbed what I could carry—an old pillow from the closet, another blanket, and the spare sheet from the spare room. When I stepped back outside, the dogs followed me to the porch, tails thumping slowly. They were my loyal shadows, no matter how much of a hot mess I was.

By the time I returned to the barn, the air was already heating from the midday sun. Dust floated through the slanted light in slow, loose spirals. He looked up when I opened the door, curiosity in his gaze.

"I brought you something," I said, setting the items down near him, bedding and a pitcher of water. "You'll be more comfortable with these."

Vek watched as I spread the blanket across the hay and tucked the pillow beneath it. When I straightened, he made that low, soft sound again—a sound that reminded me more of gratitude than anything spoken.

"Yeah," I said, my throat tightening for no good reason. "You're welcome."

He blinked slowly, his gaze following me as I turned to leave.

At the door, I paused. "If you need anything," I said without thinking, "I'll be right next door."

He tilted his head, giving the faintest nod. "Okay."

The word was rough and simple, but it stopped me cold.

I swallowed hard and forced a shaky smile. "Alright then."

When I stepped outside, the truth hit me in a quieter way.

Caring for him—checking on him, making sure he ate—felt far too natural for what he was and for everything that had happened between us last night. I didn't know what to do with that.

CHAPTER 7

Basement Confessions of a Sasquatch

Olivia

By nightfall, the ridge had vanished behind a wall of clouds. The air pressed close, rain tightening the atmosphere until the ridge felt ready to break. Every few minutes, the sky flickered—a brief, silent pulse—before thunder rolled long and low across the valley.

The day had stretched thin, slow, and uneasy. I had pretended to work, my eyes fixed on my laptop while the cursor blinked against an empty page. No matter how hard I tried, my thoughts kept straying to the barn, to Vek, and to the quiet way everything felt different with him so close.

He hadn't made a sound since morning—no movement, no hum. But I had felt him there. I had taken him food and water twice, both times leaving before courage turned into curiosity. He had eaten. That was enough, or it should have been.

Boone and June Bug had followed me all day, uneasy shadows at my heels. They felt it too—the change in the air, the slow gathering of the storm, and something else that none of us knew how to fully realize.

By nine, the first raindrops struck the windows. A line of lightning split the horizon. I turned down the news, ignoring the crawl of red across the screen: *Tornado watch*. Those were familiar words, but my stomach tightened at the thought.

When the wind began to rise, I stepped out onto the porch. The sky had taken on the color of bruised steel, with clouds shifting in layers that breathed. My porch light buzzed against the dark, its glow catching on the mist and the wings of moths.

Boone pressed his muzzle against my leg, whining softly. The air pulsed with pressure that set every nerve on edge.

"I know," I whispered, resting a hand on his head. "I feel it too."

The thunder came again—closer now, heavier. I looked toward the barn. Through the slanting rain, I could still see the faint glow of the candle I had left burning inside—a small, trembling light against the dark.

When the wind hit, it came all at once—branches thrashed, and the woods groaned. I knew that sound; I'd lived through enough Tennessee storms to recognize the shift before the sky truly turned.

"Come on," I called, whistling to the dogs. "Basement."

Boone obeyed, heading down without hesitation, but June Bug stayed at the door, her small body rigid, gaze fixed on the barn.

My stomach twisted.

"No," I told myself firmly. "He lives outside. He'll ride it out."

A violent gust slammed into the house, rattling the windows hard enough to make me flinch.

June Bug whimpered.

"That barn is older than I am," I whispered, "and if the roof gives... or he panics and runs still hurting..."

The words died in my throat.

I couldn't pretend I didn't care. Not anymore.

Before the thought finished forming, I grabbed the door and ran into the storm.

The rain struck hard and fast, soaking through my clothes in seconds. Lightning tore the sky apart, followed by a crack that made the porch boards tremble. The dogs barked behind me, their voices sharp against the roar of the wind, but I didn't stop. All I could see was mud, thunder, and the dim outline of the barn through the rain.

The door resisted when I pulled it open, the hinges wailing in protest. He was standing when I found him, framed in silver light. The quilt had slipped from his shoulders. Water clung to Vek's hair and fur, slick and gleaming under the flashes of lightning. He must have ventured outside.

His gaze found me instantly—unblinking, steady as the eye of the storm.

"There's a bad one coming," I shouted, though the words barely carried over the wind. "You can't stay here!"

He didn't move at first; he watched me with that quiet attention of his, the kind that made talking feel optional.

I pointed toward the house. "Basement. Safe."

Something in my tone must have broken through, because he nodded once and stepped forward.

We crossed the yard together, the rain driving sideways and the wind tugging at my coat. Every footfall of his landed heavily in the soaked earth, a rhythm that matched the thunder rolling above us.

By the time we reached the porch, the world had gone white with lightning. Boone barked from below, the sound half-lost in the storm.

"This way," I said, pulling the door open and heading toward the basement. "You'll have to duck."

Hesitating at the threshold, his gaze swept the narrow stairwell that led below. The dark seemed to unsettle him, perhaps an old wariness that had learned the shape of traps.

"It's alright," I said, my voice softer now. "You're safe with me."

The words felt strange on my tongue. Clearly, after shooting him, my track record proved the opposite.

For a heartbeat, neither of us moved. Then, he ducked beneath the doorframe and followed.

The lantern light trembled as I led the way down the narrow steps. Boone and June Bug came close behind, their nails scraping against the boards.

When we reached the bottom, I set the lantern on the worktable and turned it on. He filled the space behind me. It wasn't meant for someone so large. Water dripped from his hair, tracing down his throat before falling dark against the floor.

The storm howled above, but down here, it sounded far away—almost peaceful.

The wind outside rose into a steady roar, as if the whole mountain were breathing through its teeth. Every few seconds, thunder cracked close enough to rattle the hinges on the front door. Somewhere above, the old oak beside the porch groaned in protest, its branches clawing at the siding.

Down here, the air was stagnant. The scent of stone filled the small space. Candles lined the worktable, waiting for the power outages that occurred often enough to keep me prepared. I lit one, then another, their flames trembling in the draft that slipped down the stairwell.

The basement wasn't large; it was only half-finished. A futon sat against one wall, with a stack of folded blankets nearby, and shelves lined with canned goods and storm supplies. The dogs circled once before settling down, Boone placing himself between me and the stranger who had followed me down here. I felt safe, but Vek was clearly wary.

Behind me, he stood near the bottom of the stairs, his shoulders brushing against the low beams.

"You can sit," I said, my voice softer now. "It's safe down here."

He looked at the futon, then back at me, uncertain. His hair clung to his temples, deep brown and catching the candlelight in faint gold.

"Sit," I repeated, motioning to the couch as if I were talking to a nervous animal. "Rest."

He finally did, slowly, and the old futon creaked beneath his weight. The frame groaned but held. Boone lifted his head, one ear twitching, but didn't growl. Even June Bug seemed to sense that there was no danger left in him.

Then the first flicker of the lights came before blinking out completely. The hum of the refrigerator upstairs stuttered and died, leaving behind only the wind and the rain. The storm had taken the power, just like always.

I sighed. "And there it goes."

The lantern light threw everything into shadow. I could hear my own heartbeat now, too loud in the small space.

For a long, awkward moment, Vek watched me without speaking. In that soft, wavering light, his features looked sharper, almost human—strong cheekbones, eyes deep and reflective like amber glass. The bandage I had wrapped was still clean, though his shoulder was swollen from the wound.

"We need to clean your wound and change your bandage when we can go back upstairs," I said, flinching when the wind hit the outside of the house hard enough to shake the foundation.

His gaze flicked down, then back to my face. "Better," he said, the word rough but clear.

My breath caught. "You understood that?"

He nodded once. "Some."

I wasn't sure whether to feel relieved or terrified by his seemingly increasing vocabulary. "You remember English," I said slowly.

Eyebrows lifting, he tilted his head. "English." The word came out like a question, his accent shaped by years of disuse, soft around the edges.

"That's what we're speaking," I said. "You used to know it?"

A shadow crossed his expression. His eyes drifted toward the stairs, then to the lantern again, as if the flame itself might help him find the memory. "Know... before," he murmured.

"Before what?" I asked, needing to know more about him—about his history.

He didn't answer, just shook his head, a shadow darkening his eyes. The motion made the candlelight ripple across the scars that traced his ribs and collarbone. I wanted to ask more, but the words died on my tongue.

Silence fell heavily between us. The storm above had changed its tone—less violent now but closer, as if circling. Rain hammered the roof in an uneven rhythm, with the wind pushing hard against the walls.

Boone stirred restlessly, and I reached down to calm him. "It's alright, boy."

The stranger's gaze followed the movement, lingering where my hand brushed the dog's head. Then, slowly, his attention shifted back to me.

"You... afraid," he said.

The way he said it—half question, half statement—made my throat tighten. "A little," I admitted. "Storms do that to me."

He studied me for a moment longer. "Safe," he said finally, touching his chest. "You safe."

The words were rough, but the meaning was clear.

I stared at him, unsure whether to thank him or cry. "I shot you," I whispered. "You don't have to tell me that."

He frowned, searching for the right shape of the thought. "You... afraid. I... understand."

Something inside me gave way then, a quiet cracking I hadn't realized I was holding back. I sank onto the floor beside Boone, the candlelight flickering between us.

"Guess we both made mistakes," I said softly. "But you're still here. That's what matters."

He leaned forward a little, elbows on his knees, watching me with that same patient stillness. "I understand," he said slowly.

It startled me more than any thunder. For him to give me an out for nearly killing him—an out I didn't deserve.

My heart raced. "I shouldn't have shot you."

He tapped his chest again. "I understand. Liv."

Lightning flashed above, the bright light coming in through the small window and casting his shadow across the wall.

"Thank you," I said quietly, not entirely sure for what I was grateful.

He looked at me for a long moment and then nodded once. "Welcome."

The storm stalled overhead, rain hammering the roof. Wild and unrelenting rain battered the roof above us, its rhythm as chaotic as a restless heartbeat. The flickering light softened the edges of everything it touched, blurring shadows until they seemed alive. Boone slept at my feet while June Bug lay stretched across the threshold, both dogs lulled into uneasy quiet by the thunder's slow roll.

Vek sat across from me on the futon, his massive frame too large for the narrow space, shoulders curved beneath the low ceiling. Water glistened on his skin and fur, tiny beads catching the candlelight before slipping down to darken the concrete.

"You should rest," I finally said, crossing the room to grab him a towel. "We'll be here for a while."

He studied me for a long moment, his gaze steady and searching, then looked toward the stairwell as thunder boomed overhead. "Storm loud," he said, the words rough-edged but clear enough to make my breath catch.

"Yeah," I murmured, managing a faint smile. "Loud enough to make the world feel smaller."

He tilted his head as though tasting the meaning. "Small," he echoed, the sound careful on his tongue.

"You didn't tell me how you know English." Although I didn't want to push, I *needed* to know.

For a while, silence settled between us. The rain filled it easily, drumming a slow pulse into the earth above. I could hear the faint, metallic hum of the lantern and the occasional whine of wind slipping under the door. Everything felt suspended—fragile and impossibly still—like the world had narrowed down to this small, dimly lit room.

Then, in a voice quieter than before, he said, "Woman. Before. She... sing when storm come."

The words struck something deep inside me, unexpected and tender. "A woman?"

He nodded once, his eyes going distant. "Ruth." The name fell from him like an old prayer. "She... teach me words."

My throat tightened. "She took care of you."

His eyes lifted toward mine, gold catching the candlelight. "She find me. Small." He lowered his hand to the floor, palm open, showing height like a child's. "Cold. Cry. She make warm."

The space between us seemed to change then, becoming heavier... *intimate*. The kind of silence that carried both sorrow and gratitude.

"She was good to you," I said softly. "Like a mother."

He nodded again, slower this time. "Good. Kind." His brow furrowed as though the next words cost him something. "Men come. She say—run." He hesitated, breath catching. "I run."

He didn't need to finish. I could hear what lived in the space between those words.

"I'm sorry," I whispered. "You must've loved her."

He looked at the candle, at the thin ribbon of smoke curling upward, and said quietly, "She smell like bread. Earth. Always warm." His hand pressed against his chest. "Home."

That one word landed hard—simple and sacred all at once.

"She sounds like someone worth remembering," I said.

When he looked back at me, his gaze was too soft for such a huge being. "You same," he said. "Kind."

The words stole my breath. "I'm not her."

"No," he murmured. "But same heart."

Thunder rolled overhead, softer now, the storm finally moving on. The candlelight trembled. Shadows moved along the wall in slow waves, and his eyes—dark gold, reflective, alive—found mine again and held.

"I hide long," he said after a moment, the words halting but sure. "People see. Afraid."

I nodded, the confession pulling something honest out of me. "I guess we both know how that feels."

He tilted his head slightly. "You hide?"

"Maybe not like you," I said, my voice quieter now. "But, yeah. It's easier to keep to yourself. Easier than letting anyone close enough to hurt you."

Gaze never leaving my face, he seemed to think that over. "Someone hurt you."

It wasn't really a question, but I answered anyway. "Yeah. Not the kind of hurt that leaves scars, though."

He shifted slightly, elbows resting on his knees, his tone thoughtful. "Leave other mark."

The words hit like a truth I hadn't wanted to name.

"Yeah," I said. "It does." Blowing out a breath, I pressed my hand to my chest. "Here." I rarely spoke about losing my parents, but it was something that still haunted me every day, especially living in their home.

For a long moment, neither of us spoke, but there was something unsaid in that silence—an understanding that was beginning to feel less foreign. The storm had lost its rage, the thunder retreating in slow rumbles across the ridge. Boone let out a low sigh and rolled onto his side. June Bug's tail thumped once against the floor.

Vek's voice came again, his massive hand reaching for me, but pulling away before touching me. He was more afraid to touch me than I was of his touch. "You not alone."

Gathering my own courage, I reached for him instead, touching his forearm. His muscles tensed, but he didn't pull away.

"You neither," I said, hoping he believed me.

He seemed to take that in. "Safe," he said, touching his chest, then gesturing toward me. "Both."

The warmth that stirred beneath my ribs startled me. "Yeah," I whispered. "Both."

For the first time since that night in the woods, the quiet didn't frighten me. It felt like something closer to peace.

Morning crept in slowly, filtering through the cracks above the basement door in thin, silvery threads. The storm had passed hours ago, leaving the world rinsed clean and quiet. The air smelled of damp earth and candle wax, heavy with the scent of rain that had nowhere left to fall.

For a moment, I didn't move. The stillness felt sacred—the kind of hush that follows confession. Boone snored softly near the stairs, one paw twitching in a dream. June Bug had burrowed halfway beneath a blanket, her nose pressed against Vek's knee.

He was awake.

I could tell by the way he sat—his shoulders relaxed but alert, his gaze lifted toward the narrow shaft of light above us. It gilded his hair and the curve of his arm where a bandage wrapped tightly, turning every breath he took into something alive and human.

"Storm's over," I said, my voice rough from sleep.

He turned his head toward me, a faint smile shaping his mouth. "Quiet now."

It wasn't just the words—it was the rhythm, the almost-easy way he said them. His speech was still rough, but there was more confidence in it. I smiled and pushed myself upright. "You're getting better at that."

A hint of a smile lifted the sides of his mouth. "Remember. Just... long time."

The simplicity of it hit me harder than it should have. "How long has it been since you talked to anyone?"

He thought for a moment, as if counting in years he couldn't name. "Ruth," he said finally. "Only her."

The name sat between us like a fragile thing.

"She'd be proud," I murmured. "You haven't forgotten everything she taught you."

His gaze softened. "Hard to forget... kind voice."

I looked down, tracing the edge of the blanket with my thumb. "I know what you mean."

For a while, the quiet felt almost gentle. The last of the rain dripped from the gutters outside, echoing faintly through the ceiling. Boone stirred and yawned, his collar jingling against the floorboards.

"We should get upstairs," I said at last. "See if the barn still stands."

CHAPTER 8

One Tall Drink of Trouble

Olivia

In the time since we'd left the basement, I'd showered and then offered one to Vek as well. I wasn't sure what he'd done in there, but he'd left my bathroom looking like the dang tornado had torn its way through my house, after all. The world smelled clean again once the storm had passed with that sharp sweetness the rain always left behind. I stepped onto the porch barefoot, coffee steaming in one hand, Boone and June Bug trotting ahead to inspect every puddle like they'd never seen one before.

The storm had passed sometime after dawn, leaving branches scattered across the yard and half my fence leaning like a drunk after last call. I should've been cursing about it, but the morning air carried that washed, forgiving calm that made anger feel out of place.

Behind me, the door creaked open. I didn't have to look to know who it was, which was admittedly strange.

Vek filled the doorway. The sun caught the damp strands of his hair, the faint shimmer along his arms, turning him gold at the edges.

"Fence broke," he said, his voice still rough but easier than the day before. He'd certainly gotten practice talking to me until we'd fallen asleep.

"Yeah," I said, nodding toward the damage. "Storm took half of it."

"I fix," he said simply, stepping onto the porch.

"You don't have to—"

He was already moving past me.

"—help," I finished weakly. "Right. Why listen to the woman who shot you?"

Although he didn't speak a reply, he gave an amused sound in his throat, like laughter that hadn't learned to be loud yet. Boone barked once in agreement and darted toward the fallen fence-post. June Bug followed, tail wagging like it might take flight.

"Fence's split clean through," I said, kneeling to check the splintered beam.

Before I could reach for it, Vek crouched beside me. His shadow crossed over mine as he wrapped one massive hand around the post and lifted it as if it weighed nothing.

"Well, damn," I muttered.

He looked over, eyes questioning. "Bad?"

"Impressive," I admitted. I'd thought Gunner was strong, especially with a little Jack in him, but Vek could probably benchpress my brother on a bad day. No contest.

He studied me for a moment, then the corner of his mouth twitched. "Good," he said, and set the post upright as though the rest of it wasn't strewn all over the yard.

Boone barked again, thrilled to have a new member of their pack. June Bug dragged a stick twice her size across the grass, tail spinning like a fan.

"Real team effort," I said, brushing dirt from my hands. "One man-mountain, two idiots, and me."

Vek tilted his head. "Not idiot," he said, looking at the dogs.

"Trust me," I replied, "you haven't seen them when I pull out the vacuum cleaner." Although I realized he probably didn't know what a vacuum cleaner was.

He huffed—almost laughter. It startled me how easily it came now.

The wind shifted, carrying the scent of wet pine and the faint sweetness of smoke from somewhere down the ridge. He glanced toward it, the sunlight catching along his jaw.

"Storm loud," he said quietly. "But quiet after feels...good."

"Peaceful," I offered, taking in a deep breath.

He nodded slowly, testing the word. "Peaceful."

Never in my wildest dreams did I ever see myself teaching a Sasquatch to talk, but for the first time in what felt like forever, I didn't feel like running or apologizing. I just stood there, the grass damp under my feet, watching sunlight break through the clouds while a myth fixed my fence like it was the most ordinary thing in the world.

By the time we'd done clearing the fence line, the sun had burned off the last of the mist. Boone flopped in the grass, tongue hanging, and June Bug chased a butterfly she'd never catch. I turned toward the porch, already picturing hot coffee and dry clean clothes—then froze.

Right behind me, Vek stood naked as the day he was born. In that dark basement light, I hadn't given it a thought. But if he planned to park his butt on my good furniture, he'd need cover... and all the other bits flappin' in the breeze made it hard to focus.

"Oh, Lord have mercy—no." I jabbed a finger at the steps. "You ain't goin' back in the barn, but you're gonna need clothes first."

He paused, one hand on the rail, head tilted like I'd lost my tongue.

"Clothes," I said, waving at him. "Gotta have 'em. Pants. Like... today."

He frowned. "Not cold."

"Doesn't matter," I said, shaking my head. "It's a people thing."

He stared a beat longer, unconvinced.

"Stay," I said, pointing at the porch like I was training some enormous, well-behaved wolf.

Boone barked once, as if in agreement.

Inside, I rifled through the hall closet till I dug up a pair of Gunner's old pajama pants—faded flannel, frayed cuffs, survivor of too many hunts. They'd suffice.

When I came back, Vek was inspecting my wind chime like it held the secrets of the universe.

"Here," I said, tossing him the pants. "Ain't perfect, but they'll keep the wildlife from filing complaints."

He caught them carefully, fingers tracing the threads. "These... go on legs?"

"That's the plan."

He nodded, face grave, and eased one leg in, then the other. The waistband straining for dear life, cuffs skimming his ankles, but by some miracle, it looked... *decent*.

"Too short," he grunted.

"Well, they're your only choice, so congrats—you're on the cutting edge of Sasquatch fashion."

He cracked a small smile—an almost-smile that threw me for a loop.

"You hungry?" I asked, spinning before he could read my face. "Might as well put some food in you before noon."

His jaw shifted, understanding softening his features. "Food good."

Something stirred in my chest. Maybe curiosity, maybe trouble; I couldn't say which. "Pancakes okay?" I asked, clearing my throat. "Got some mix in the cupboard."

He peered at the kitchen, then back at me. "You make for me?"

That hit me harder than a bucking colt. "Guess I do."

Vek nodded once. "I eat all."

I shook my head, already mentally counting the eggs left in my fridge. "Reckon my grocery bill's about to double."

The kitchen was quiet except for the slow tick of the pilot flame and the scrape of a skillet over the burner. Morning light slipped through the window. With no power, the room felt old-fashioned, like it remembered life before the world got so damn loud. Back when Mamma and Daddy were still the ones cooking in the kitchen.

Grief threatened to rear its ugly head instead of nostalgia, but I pushed it back and took a sip of my tea.

Vek sat by the window, elbows on knees, taking up his space like he owned it. Boone lay beside his chair, tail thumping now and then, while June Bug snored under the table, paws twitching after invisible rabbits.

"You've got yourself a fan club," I said, flipping a pancake. "They think you hung the moon."

He cocked his head. "Fan... club?"

"Means they like you more than me," I said. "But don't go big-headed on me."

He cracked a half-smile. "Big head," he repeated, tapping his temple. "Got one."

I laughed, and the sound filled the small kitchen, making everything feel right again. Big head, big feet. He was big all around. I was just glad I got pants on him, but they were admittedly more for my benefit than his.

When I cracked an egg, he leaned closer, brow furrowed as the yolk spread in the pan. "Egg," he said, slow and careful.

I nodded, feeling a little too much like I was a kindergarten teacher standing before a big, hairy student who'd been held back way too many times. "Impressive memory."

"Food?"

"Breakfast," I said. "A sacred human ceremony involving sugar and serious denial."

He thought on that, then nodded. "I like breakfast."

"Most important meal," I said. "That's what they say."

Butter hissed in the heat, turning sweet and rich. He inhaled like it was the best thing he'd ever smelled.

"Fire makes food," he said.

"Fire makes everything better," I said, flipping the pancake. "Well... almost everything."

His eyes caught mine. "What not better?"

The question felt like an invitation. "Some things you don't need hotter," I murmured, turning away before my cheeks burned.

I slid the pancake onto a plate. "Alright, breakfast of champions. You ever used a fork?"

He studied the fork as if it were alien tech. "Stick with teeth?"

"Works for me."

Brow furrowed, he stabbed at the pancake awkwardly, but I only let him hack away at his food for a few seconds before I reached over to guide his hand. My fingers brushed his, his hand warm and calloused.

"Like this," I murmured, trying to redirect my attention. "Stab it, don't crush it."

He tried again, focusing as if he were playing chess. When he finally bit down, his eyes went wide, then softened.

"Sweet," he said at last, syrup dripping down his chin.

"Sugar." I grinned. "Dangerous stuff."

He nodded, still chewing. "I like danger."

I blinked, feeling heat rise to my cheeks. "Is that so?" The words came out softer than intended, caught somewhere between teasing and genuine curiosity.

His chest vibrated with something like laughter—a deep, quiet sound that seemed to travel through the floorboards. Boone's ears perked up at the rumble, his tail sweeping once across the wood before he settled back into his dreams.

When I slid another pancake onto Vek's plate, he set his fork down. The syrup still lingered on his chin, catching the morning light. "You eat too," he said, pointing at my empty plate.

Smiling, I lifted my fork. "I will." Truth was, watching him discover breakfast had made me forget my own hunger.

"Good," he said, nodding firmly at the table. "Eat. Talk. Laugh." He tapped the wooden surface with one thick finger. "Makes home."

Something inside me twisted helplessly. "Yeah," I said, throat suddenly tight. "It does."

He studied me for a long moment, then cracked a real smile. It started small at the corner of his mouth, then reached his eyes, crinkling the thick skin.

"What?" I asked.

"You happy now."

It wasn't a question.

I laughed, because it was either that or cry. "Reckon I might be."

Leaning back in the chair, he draped one arm over its back like he'd been sitting at kitchen tables his whole damn life. Boone snored louder. June Bug twitched. The whole house seemed to exhale.

"You keep lookin' at me like that," I warned, "and I'll forget you were ever supposed to be the big scary monster in these woods."

He cocked his head, thoughtful. "Forget good?"

"Depends on what you're forgettin'."

As if that made perfect sense, he nodded. "Then I stay little bit monster. Easier to remember."

That earned another laugh, and I didn't bother hiding it.

The air had grown heavy again by afternoon, sunlight thick enough to taste. Every blade of grass still held a damp shine from the torrential rain. I'd spent most of the day patching what the storm had bullied—tightening loose hinges on the screen door, sweeping debris, pretending I wasn't watching the man who shadowed me from one task to the next.

Vek worked without asking what needed doing. He hauled branches that looked half his size, reset a fencepost that had given up the ghost, and ignored every warning I threw his way about resting. His wound from where I'd shot him was healing, but the last thing I wanted was for him to reopen it.

"Alright, hero," I called, tossing the hammer onto the porch. "You're done."

He straightened, the mud on his fur telling me he would need another shower. Although after the mess he'd made that morning, I was thinking about just hosing him off in the yard. "Fence still broken."

"Fence can wait," I said, pointing toward the porch. "You sit before you start leaking blood again."

That earned the faintest flicker of amusement, but he obeyed, lowering himself onto the step with care. The wood creaked but held. His long legs stretched out before him, big bare feet leaving prints in the mud. I went inside to fetch clean bandages. Ever my loyal shadow, Boone followed, toenails clicking a beat behind me.

When I came back, Vek was watching June Bug chase a butterfly in slow, dizzy circles. His eyes softened in a way I'd never seen before.

"Hold still," I said, kneeling beside him. "Let's get this cleaned off."

He looked down at me instead. "You fix again?"

"That's what I do." Careful not to touch the raw edge of the wound, I unwound the bandage. It had healed faster than I expected, which was a small blessing.

"You heal fast," I said. "Show-off."

He made a low sound in his chest, something halfway between laughter and a hum. The vibration rolled through the air and into my hands.

"Keep this up, and I'll have to hide the hammer just to make sure you rest."

"Hide from me?" he asked, eyes glinting.

"Hide the hammer, not me." I tied the new bandage snug and glanced up. "Although maybe I should. You'd never sit still if I didn't keep you in one place."

He tilted his head, curiosity flickering in his eyes. "You like when I sit?"

"Yeah," I said, smiling before I could stop myself. "Means I get to breathe."

He looked at my mouth then, just for a second too long, and the air changed. The easy rhythm between us wavered, caught somewhere between safety and something riskier.

I cleared my throat and stood. "No heavy lifting until tomorrow. Doctor's orders."

"Doctor?" he echoed.

"Someone who fixes people. Like I'm fixing you."

"Then you are doctor," he said.

"Lord help us all," I muttered.

The corner of his mouth twitched, that almost-smile that had started to feel like my favorite bad habit.

The light stretched long across the yard, softening to honey. Boone flopped into the grass, June Bug claiming his belly as her pillow. Somewhere down the ridge, someone's chimney sent up a thin coil of smoke.

Vek tipped his head back to look at the sky. "Pretty," he said.

"Yeah." I followed his gaze. "It's a good kind of quiet today."

He nodded, slow and thoughtful. "Quiet not always bad."

"No," I said softly. "Not anymore."

I sank onto the porch swing, the chain complaining but holding. Vek remained where he was on the top step, his knees bent, shoulders relaxed. He looked less like a stranger now—still something out of legend, but no longer elusive. The more he talked to me, the more I realized just how like me he was. Hollyweird had Sasquatch all wrong—at least my Sasquatch. Mine? Nope. *Goodness help me.*

For a long time, we sat quietly, the creak of the swing nearly putting me to sleep. Then Boone's head snapped up. He lifted his nose to the air and let out a long, lonely howl that echoed through the hollow, making a flock of birds flee from the trees like something from a horror flick.

"Don't you dare," I warned, already seeing the thought flash across Vek's face, but before the words entirely left my mouth, Vek tilted his head toward the rising moon and joined in, his voice like some kind of werewolf. The sound rolled across the yard, shaking the porch boards. Boone barked mid-note, thrilled by the duet. It only took a second for June Bug to join in. Make that three idiots and me.

I tried to scold him, but laughter hit so hard I had to bend over. "Stop! Lord, stop! The whole ridge is gonna think I'm keeping wolves."

Quieting, he watched me with that half-smile that had started to feel dangerous. "Funny," he said.

Still laughing, I nodded. "I think you're trouble."

That earned another crooked smile. "Good trouble."

"Can't argue with that," I said, wiping the tears from my eyes.

Everything settled again, soft and gold under the last stretch of daylight. Fireflies blinked near the porch, their small lights weaving between the boards.

"Guess you're officially part of the pack now," I said, my laugh finally fading.

He considered that for a moment, then nodded. "Good pack," he said simply.

Something eased inside me, although I was afraid of what that meant. "Yeah," I murmured. "Good pack."

The swing kept its slow rhythm, Boone sighed from his patch of grass, and Vek sat near enough that his warmth reached me through the cooling air. It wasn't the kind of quiet that asked for space. It was the kind that felt like home.

CHAPTER 9

Dial M for Mythical Boyfriend

Olivia

A week had passed since the storm, and the house had fallen into Vek's rhythm. Two mugs waited on the counter every morning—mine, and the chipped one with faded cats that had quietly become his. The coffeepot hissed like it had opinions, filling the kitchen with the smell of dark roast and something close to peace.

Sprawled under the table, Boone sighed in his sleep. June Bug sprawled on the rug, paws twitching at whatever ghost she chased in her head. Down the hall, one particular floorboard gave its familiar groan under Vek's weight as he walked toward the shower. That sound had joined the place like it belonged—a heartbeat too big for the frame, but essential to it now. He'd taken over the guest room, and even though his shoulder was healing clean, I couldn't picture that room empty again without feeling wrong.

The phone buzzed against the counter, sharp in the quiet.

"Morning, brother of mine," I said, pinning it between my ear and shoulder while I poured cream into my mug. "You don't usually call this early. What's wrong?"

"Nothing yet," Gunner said. His voice came rough, all gravel and not enough sleep. We hadn't talked since his birthday stunt on the ridge. "You heard from T-Bone lately?"

A humorless breath slipped out. "Is that a trick question? Haven't seen him since he borrowed my ladder and never brought it back."

T-Bone had shown up two days after the storm, swaggering on my porch like always. Vek had been inside, thank God, but that near miss still sat heavy behind my ribs. I got rid of T-Bone fast. The part I couldn't figure out was how to make that permanent.

Gunner chuckled, but there wasn't much warmth in it. "You're better off. He's been actin' a damn fool, tellin' anybody who'll listen about the beast on the ridge. Tryin' to rile folks up."

"Oh, for heaven's sake." The creamer hit the counter harder than it needed to. "He's preachin' Sasquatch again?"

Even though Gunner and I both knew Vek was real—we'd both been there that first night on the ridge when Vek had made contact—I hadn't told him about the way Vek had followed me home. Or about the bullet. Or the barn. Or the guest room. We were close, but I had no idea how he'd react to "By the way, the legend lives in my house now." I sure didn't want half the county stomping into my valley like it was a field trip. And I certainly wasn't down for a Redneck Beauty and the Beast remake.

"Louder than ever," Gunner said. "He's tryin' to drag people back up there with him. Says this is his redemption."

"That man couldn't redeem a coupon." The coffee bit sharp, then settled warm in my chest. My mind was already ahead of him. They wouldn't find Vek on the ridge anymore—but they might discover signs he existed. Tracks. Hair. A broken branch line that pointed downhill. A trail that ended in my yard.

"Yeah, well, he's convinced somebody's gonna listen. I told him I was out." Paper rustled on the other end—his desk, his shift, his life back in the city. "Didn't take it well."

"You finally quit babysittin' him? I'm proud of you," I said, though the air in the room had started to feel too thin. "You think he's really heading back up there?"

"Probably. He can't stand bein' ordinary. Folks like him talk too loud until somebody gets hurt. Just thought you should know I'm steering clear for a while. He's wound tight, Liv. Tight enough to snap."

"Good," I said, even as something tightened under my sternum. "Let him chase shadows. Maybe he'll tire himself out."

Maybe he'll find a trail. Maybe he'll follow it. I didn't say any of that. Thinking it once was bad enough.

"Maybe," Gunner said. Another shuffle of papers. "You doin' alright up there?"

"Fine. Fence is mended, dogs are happy, coffee's strong. What could go wrong?"

"That's my girl," he said, softer now. "Keep it that way."

"I'll do my best."

He hesitated. "Call me if you need anything. And if T-Bone starts flappin' that mouth near you, don't engage. Let him talk himself dry."

"Copy that, Sergeant Buzzkill."

"Always tryin'."

The line clicked. the kitchen went still again—the soft tick of the cooling pot, Boone's lazy sigh under the table, the distant rush of the shower cutting off down the hall. The air tightened, the way it does before a front moves in. I rubbed the heel of my hand against my chest, where the worry had started to settle like storm pressure.

A floorboard creaked behind me.

Vek filled the doorway, a towel slung around his shoulders. His fur was still damp where it framed his face and collarbone. The extra-*extra*-large jogging pants I'd ordered online hung low on his hips; even so, they were fighting for the right to exist. He made the kitchen look small and fragile just by standing in it.

"Bad voice?" he asked.

"Not bad," I said, forcing my shoulders to drop. "Just my brother—worried about a friend who's gettin' himself in trouble."

"Trouble," he repeated slowly. He tasted the word like something he didn't trust yet. "Means...not good?"

"Exactly." I nudged the second mug toward him. "Let's hope he finds some sense." If I held my breath waiting on that, they'd find me blue on the floor.

Steam drifted up between us. He watched it a moment before he asked, "Your brother—good man?"

"The best kind," I said. "Loud, stubborn, always right even when he's not. Runs in the family."

That pulled a hint of a smile from him. He wrapped his hand around the mug like it was nothing, even though it barely fit. "Coffee," he said.

"Careful—it's hot."

He drank anyway, eyes on me over the rim. Curiosity lived there now, settled deep. Not just about the house or the words, but about me. A seven-foot myth in too-tight sweatpants drinking from a chipped cat mug wasn't anywhere on my life plan, but somehow he'd started to fit. The air between us felt charged, but I did my best to push past it.

"Trouble's a talker," I said under my breath. "It'll find its way down the mountain soon enough."

His gaze slid past me to the kitchen window, where the ridge rose dark against a pale sky. For a moment, he just listened, shoulders gone still in a way that had nothing to do with the house.

"Then we go up," he said.

I blinked. "Go up where?"

He nodded toward the ridge. "There. I show you. How I live before. How I find food."

My pulse stuttered. "You mean now?"

"Yes," he said. "Good day. No storm." His eyes narrowed slightly, like he was reading the weather in some language I didn't speak. "You learn."

The argument lined up in my head—too risky and too far—but the way he said it pressed against all of that. You learn. Not a command. An offer.

My mug landed on the counter with a soft clink. "Fine," I said. "But if this ends with me face-down in the mud or chased by a bear, I'm hauntin' you."

The corner of his mouth lifted. "You try."

"Lord help me," I muttered, reaching for my jacket. "You sound like my brother already."

The word brother caught his attention again. He tilted his head, as if filing it away for later, then crossed to the door. When he opened it, he stepped aside and waited, big hand resting light on the frame.

"Come," he said. "We go."

Cool air slipped into the kitchen, carrying the faint, sharp promise of a front still too far off to see. I looked at the open doorway, at him, at the life I'd somehow let inside my house, and stepped through first.

The woods behind my property weren't strangers to me, but walking into them with Vek at my side made them feel sharpened around the edges—familiar paths carrying a different kind of weight. He didn't take the trail. He moved beside it, quiet as a cat, slipping between trees like he'd been carved from the same grain. Sunlight broke through the canopy in patches across the trails, catching on the broad line of his back.

Boone trotted ahead with the confidence of a dog who believed he led expeditions. June Bug zigzagged between us, convinced she'd discovered every stick that ever existed in the history of creation.

"What exactly are we doing?" I asked, stepping over a slick branch.

He didn't slow. "Show."

"Show what?"

He cast me a quick glance—just enough to catch the faint curve at the corner of his mouth. "How I live."

That shouldn't have rattled me, but it did. I tried to keep my eyes on the uneven ground instead of on the way sunlight slid across his shoulders. If my mama could see me now.

"You're not about to chase down a deer in front of me," I said. "Because I'm not emotionally prepared for that before lunch."

"Too loud," he said. "No chase. We watch."

The word we did something to my balance, but I pushed it away and focused on the trees instead.

"We watch," I repeated. "And after watching?"

"Catch."

I shook my head. "Of course. So civilized."

His gaze dipped to my boots. "Vek. No guns."

That hit with the kind of accuracy I wished I didn't admire. Guilt pricked at the edges. "Yeah," I muttered. "That's fair. If I shoot another mythical creature this year, I'm just gonna move to Florida and bartend for the snowbirds."

A low rumble rolled from his chest—a laugh, or the closest thing he had to one.

The deeper we went, the quieter the forest grew. Birds stilled overhead. The air shifted too—lighter but charged, the faint metallic edge that always arrived before a storm thought about gathering itself. Vek noticed first. His ears twitched, his head tilting up.

"Wind changes," he said.

"Storm coming?"

"Later." His voice settled low. "Not now."

It didn't comfort me as much as I'd hoped. Springs could be ferocious with storms, and I didn't want to get caught in one.

Several minutes later, we slipped into a clearing where a narrow stream cut through the earth—clear, cold, singing over stone. Vek crouched near the edge and motioned for me to follow. Boone splashed upstream immediately. June Bug barked at her reflection and scared herself. *A mountain man, two idiots, and me, once again.*

Vek dipped his fingers into the current, eyes tracking the shadows beneath the water. "Here," he murmured.

I crouched beside him, knees easing into damp moss. "Here what—"

Then I saw it: a flicker of silver darting below the surface.

"Fish," I whispered.

He nodded. "Fast. Watch."

I opened my mouth to ask why we were crouched like cryptids in a nature documentary, but before the thought finished forming, his hand shot forward silently, and came back with a trout flipping wildly against his palm.

"Lord have mercy," I breathed, half-laughing. "You didn't even scare it."

As though it were just another day, he examined it and then released it gently before shaking the water from his fingers. "Too small."

"How long do we wait?"

"Until ready."

"Is that your whole philosophy?"

He smiled, the corners of his eyes crinkling. "It works."

So, we waited, but the quiet around us wasn't empty; it listened. The scent of crushed leaves followed our steps and the faintest thread of weather coming from far down the ridge. A kind of stillness pulled between us.

"You quiet," he said after a moment, catching me by surprise. I'd been twisting wildflowers into a bracelet, lost in my own thoughts.

"I'm thinking."

"Good or bad?"

"That depends. You want the truth or the polite version?"

He didn't hesitate. "Truth."

Setting the flowers down, I let a breath slip out. "I'm thinking this is the strangest date I've ever been on."

He blinked. "Date?"

"When two people spend time together on pur-pose," I said, acutely aware of the heat in my face. "Usually not... like this."

His mouth softened at the edges. "You laugh more now."

I didn't look at him. Didn't trust myself to. "Maybe I just needed a change of scenery." A beat passed. "Or company."

A flash of silver cut the water again. Vek moved impossibly fast. The trout broke the surface in his grasp, larger this time and thrashing with all its might.

"Dinner," he said.

Although I grimaced, I leaned in to look closer. "You're serious."

"Yes."

He didn't hand it over immediately—he studied me first, like he was checking for something be-neath my expression. Then he offered it. The fish slapped my wrist as I grabbed it.

"Vek!" I yelped, barely keeping his catch contained.

His warm laugh rolled through the clearing, pulling straight through my chest. "Trade," he said. "You teach words. I teach this."

I tried to glare, but failed. "Fine. But next time we're doing pancakes. Less... flopping."

He watched me like the sunlight and the smile I was fighting were somehow the same thing. "Good," he said softly. "You laugh."

Something inside me folded at the words. Something I was afraid to admit.

As I warred with my emotions, he rose and offered his hand. His palm was broad and warm, the kind of hold that didn't ask for trust but earned it. I took it without question.

"Come," he said. "Home."

For a heartbeat, everything stilled—the charged air, the stream, my breath. Then I nodded. "Yeah," I whispered. "Let's go home."

By the time we reached the house, clouds stacked low over the ridge. Clouds stacked low and dark, heavy enough to feel in my teeth. Boone trotted ahead as he always did, carrying his stick like he'd discovered fire. June Bug waddled in crooked circles behind him, worn out from saving the world.

Vek walked beside me, quiet, the trout hanging from his hand as if it weighed nothing at all. The air tasted metallic—storm-breeding weather—and the first threads of wind teased at the leaves along the tree line.

Inside, the house held the lingering scene of coffee. I set the pan on the counter and lit the burner, the flame catching with a soft whump. Vek stood near the window, watching the sky the way some folks study scripture.

"You felt it earlier," I said, seasoning the fish.

"Yes." His voice stayed low. "Storm comes fast."

"Always does this time of year." I glanced toward the ridge. "She's just gettin' warmed up."

A low roll of thunder answered, stretching too long, and the windows rattled with it. Boone froze under the table, and June Bug crawled directly onto Vek's foot like he was the only high ground left. They had become quite attached to him.

He glanced down at her, then back at the sky. "They feel it," he said.

"Yeah," I murmured. "So do I."

The room filled with the smell of crisping skin and pine smoke. I'd cooked fish a thousand times, but somehow this felt different—like the storm and the silence and the man-thing watching me all braided together under the same roof.

Abandoning the window, he drifted closer to the stove, curiosity softening the lines between his brows. "You cook fish much?"

"Not usually what I catch with my bare hands," I said, flipping the fish. "But yeah. I've cooked it before."

Another rumble rolled over the ridge, closer this time. The storm had picked up speed. Wind pressed against the windows, setting my nerves buzzing.

"Where did you stay during storms when you were out there?" I asked. Just the thought of him being hunched over in the rain, cold and alone, brought a sting to the backs of my eyes.

Vek glanced toward the window again, eyes going distant. "Caves."

Lightning flashed—no sound yet, just a white vein in the clouds. The reflection lit the fur along his shoulders, turning him into something carved from weather instead of bone.

"You don't have to do that anymore," I said softly. "Be out there alone."

He didn't look away from the window. "You want that?"

My heart tripped. "Want what?"

When he turned toward me, I could tell by the look in his eyes that he was choosing the moment carefully. "Me staying."

The thunder waited for my answer.

Swallowing hard, I dipped my chin. "I want you safe. That's all."

"Safe here." He said it like he was putting something together, like a truth was brushing against the edges of his understanding.

I didn't trust my voice, so I checked the fish instead. "Dinner's ready."

We ate at the counter while the storm pushed across the sky. Rain tapped lightly at first—a polite knock—then shifted into a steadier beat. The dogs edged closer until all four of us were crowded at the same end of the kitchen.

Lightning cracked somewhere too close. The lights blinked once, then gave up entirely.

Darkness swallowed the house, and I froze. No matter how old I got, storms always made me feel like a frightened child.

Rain hit the roof hard enough to drown out thought.

In the dark, Vek stood and crossed the room, finding the counter, then the drawer with the matches. A faint scratch, then the tiny flare of flame lit his face in gold.

"You okay?" he asked, lighting a candle.

"Yeah," I said, though my heartbeat disagreed. "Just... don't love the dark when the wind gets ideas."

Lightning flashed through the kitchen window—bright enough to paint his silhouette in white for a heartbeat. He didn't even blink. Instead, he stepped closer, lowering the candle so the glow settled between us.

"You safe," he said again, his knuckles brushing my face, "Here."

The touch lingered, sending goosebumps across my body. Part of me knew I wanted more, but I wasn't ready to admit it yet.

Using the candle, I lit a lamp, and warm light pushed back the dark. Rain hammered harder against the roof, and the walls creaked under the wind.

"Will rain a lot," he said, patting June Bug on the head.

"Probably," I said. "Depends which way she turns."

As the words settled between us, I realized I wasn't just talking about the weather.

CHAPTER 10

The Drunk on the Porch

Olivia

Storms always left the ridge too quiet afterward. The kind of quiet that didn't belong to peace—more like the world hadn't quite decided whether it was done shaking. Rain still clung to the eaves in slow, stubborn drops. The fire I'd banked earlier gave the room a tired glow, soft enough that the shadows didn't try to misbehave.

Boone stretched near the hearth, chin on his paws, and June Bug snored under Vek's chair.

Vek stayed close without pressing in, his heat drifting toward me. His presence settled into the corners in a way nothing else ever had.

The knock broke everything.

Soft at first—too soft for the hour.

Boone shot to his feet with a bark that cracked straight through the quiet. June Bug startled, her growl wobbling out like she'd borrowed it from a much larger dog.

The second knock hit harder. A dull thud that rattled the frame.

I stood, mug forgotten, one hand hovering near the door without touching it. The house stilled around me. Even the rain seemed to hold its breath. I heard Vek rise behind me.

"Who's there?" My voice tried for firm and only halfway succeeded.

A slurred drawl seeped through the wood. "Evenin', Liv. Didn't mean to wake ya."

T-Bone.

"You sure as hell didn't aim to let me sleep, bangin' on my door this late," I said, my stomach dropping into something cold and hollow. "You're drunk. Go home."

He laughed. It was mean, ugly, the kind you only heard when he'd had one too many. "Heard you weren't alone out here. Thought I'd come say hello."

Hackles up, Boone wedged himself between me and the door, teeth bared at a man he'd never trusted. His small body shook behind the closed door with the effort of looking bigger than he was.

Although he remained silent, Vek stepped into the lamplight near the window. His shadow stretched long across the floorboards, bending the small room around him.

"You need to leave, T-Bone," I repeated. "It's late."

"That him in there?" His voice lifted, ugly with suspicion. "You got some fella hidin' in these hills? Or..." A thick snort. "Maybe it ain't a man at all."

The air in the room thinned.

Vek moved closer. That simple shift changed the whole house—the dogs went silent, the fire dimmed, even my pulse paused to listen.

Then the door jerked. It wasn't a knock. The damned fool was trying to force his way inside.

"Open up, Liv," T-Bone slurred. "Don't act like you've got somethin' to hide."

The push snapped something inside me—fear, anger, instinct all crashing at once. My breath hitched; my feet moved back without asking me.

Without saying a word, Vek stepped past me.

He didn't growl. Didn't show teeth. He simply wrapped his hand around the lock and turned. Metal complained under his grip.

Lightning cracked across the yard, lighting him up in a hard, white flash.

T-Bone leaned in too close, rain dripping from his chin, irritation twisting his mouth like he meant to shove the door again.

Then he saw Vek.

Not all at once—his drunk brain tried to make sense of the size first, then the shape, then the wrongness of the silhouette filling the doorway. His hand—raised a second ago to pound on the frame again—hovered in midair, wavering.

"What—" he started, the word slurred with confusion.

Vek growled.

Not loud.

A low, rumbling vibration that lifted from deep in his chest—so deep it moved through the floorboards and curled straight up my spine. Boone froze mid-bark. June Bug went silent. Even the storm seemed to stall mid-breath.

T-Bone blinked, then instinct dragged him a half-step back, like he suddenly wasn't sure where the safe distance was.

Vek stepped forward.

One slow, heavy shift that brought him out of the doorway and onto the porch. Rain hit him instantly, sliding through his hair, catching on the broad lines of his shoulders. Standing fully in the storm, he looked larger... older... closer to whatever the ridge had whispered about before I ever knew his name.

Eyes widening, T'Bone's throat bobbed in a hard swallow.

Then Vek growled again—deeper this time, a sound meant for warning, not violence, but vicious enough to hit bone.

As though God had a sense of humor, thunder cracked overhead, shaking the windows.

T-Bone screamed.

A raw, panicked scream that tore out of him as he jerked backward, boots slipping on the wet steps. He hit the mud, scrambled up on hands and knees, breath stuttering in terrified bursts as he clawed his way toward the truck.

He didn't look back. Not once.

Just bolted—slipping, scrambling—until he dove into the driver's seat and fishtailed down the gravel drive, engine shrieking like he believed something was chasing him.

For the first time in his whole sorry life, T-Bone finally understood he wasn't the biggest monster on this mountain.

My fingers ached from clinging to the frame. Creeping forward, Boone sniffed Vek's ankle, then pressed himself protectively beside him.

Vek didn't move from the doorway. His chest lifted slowly, drawing in the last of the storm-scent. Rain clung to his hair in tiny beads of lamplight.

"You didn't... hurt him," I managed.

He shook his head. "Only scare."

"That's one way to put it." The words scraped out thin. My knees were still locked in place, and I couldn't remember when I'd stopped breathing.

I peeled my hand off the doorframe slowly, fingers stiff, knuckles aching from how hard I'd braced myself. Boone crept forward on cautious paws, sniffing the spot where T-Bone had stood, but even he kept glancing back at Vek like he wasn't sure what he'd just witnessed.

My heartbeat hammered too close to my throat.

"I've never heard that man scream." The sentence shook more than I wanted it to. The room still felt unsettled, like the storm had pushed it sideways and hadn't bothered to set it right again.

"That was…" I swallowed hard, trying to steady my breath. "That was a lot."

The air carried the scent of rain and fear and something older—whatever had rolled off Vek when he stepped into the storm. My hands still trembled from the sight of it, from how quickly the moment turned, from how close the whole damn thing came to breaking wide open.

"I thought he was going to push his way in," I whispered. "I thought—God, Vek, I didn't know what he'd do."

My chest tightened again, dread taking up space there.

"And I didn't know what you were going to do either."

Vek finally turned. The light caught his eyes, softening the gold. "He came when you said no."

"That doesn't always mean danger." My throat thickened. "Sometimes he's just—stubborn. Loud."

"He pushed door."

The truth of it cracked straight through every excuse I had left.

"Yeah," I whispered. "He did."

Boone pressed against my leg. I steadied a hand on his neck.

When Vek moved closer, it was in mindful inches, each shift weighed against my fear. His gaze dropped to my trembling hands.

"You shake," he said quietly.

"It's adrenaline. It'll go."

"Fear?"

"Not of you." The honesty came too fast to take back, but it was God's honest truth.

A small change moved through him—jaw easing, shoulders loosening as though something inside him softened in response.

"He has been close before?" he asked.

I shrugged. "T-Bone? Close enough to make me uncomfortable. Close enough Boone stepped between us. But he's never touched me."

A tightness pulled at Vek's jaw.

"He would have."

Although I was scared to admit it, I didn't deny it. I couldn't.

A quiet shift passed between us then—an understanding.

Vek stepped toward me. He certainly could be imposing, but he didn't tower. He didn't loom. Instead, he moved with the care of someone approaching something precious. Warmth radiated from him, brushing my arms, my throat, the narrow space between our breaths.

"Olivia."

My name carried intention, carefully shaped, offered with tenderness beneath it.

"Yeah." The word was just a whisper, my chest too tight to do more.

His hand lifted hesitantly, asking without words. His fingertips brushed my cheek, gentle enough that my breath almost broke. The touch was warm. Careful. *Restrained.*

"I protect you always."

"I know."

Not daring to say more, I bit my lip, and Vek's gaze drifted to my mouth, something warm and dawning moving behind his eyes.

I didn't step back. I didn't breathe.

"Vek," I whispered.

The realization that hit me at that moment must have struck him as well, because as though he read my mind, he leaned in—just enough that his breath touched my lips. "I want to... do right."

Lifting my hand, I touched his chest, hard muscle beneath soft fur. "You are."

His forehead brushed mine, and then he kissed me.

The first press of his mouth was careful. Testing. Like every part of him was braced to pull away the second I flinched. His lips were warm against mine, soft in a way that didn't match the rest of him at all, and a low sound rolled up from his chest—half breath, half need.

Fire rushed through me so quickly it felt like my body had been waiting for him without admitting it. My hands curled into his shoulders, fingers sinking into damp fur and solid muscle. He held himself so gently, every line of him braced as though one wrong move might send me slipping away.

He drew back a fraction, eyes searching my face like he already knew the answer but had to hear it anyway. "Right?" he murmured.

I swallowed, breath shaky and full in my throat. "Right," I whispered. "Very right."

His posture softened. A tiny shift in the set of his shoulders, a softening at the corner of his mouth. His hand slid into my hair, fingers threading through with slow, careful strokes, and he kissed me again.

The second kiss carried more intent.

When his thumb grazed the hinge of my jaw, coaxing my lips open, heat pooled low in my belly, spreading outward in a warm, unsteady sweep. My knees wobbled; if he hadn't been holding me, the floor would've had me.

Beside us, Boone gave a long, unimpressed huff and flopped down in front of the hearth. June Bug buried her face under a pillow like she'd made a decision to opt out of whatever this was.

The room tightened around us, smaller and warmer, like the only place that mattered was the breath between our mouths.

"Olivia," he murmured, my name rolling slowly over his tongue, still new to him but spoken with such care that it scattered something inside me.

"Yeah," I whispered, my voice catching. "I'm here."

His forehead rested against mine for a heartbeat, his breath brushing my lips. "I want..." He paused, searching for the words. "I want you safe. I want..." His brow furrowed. "Right."

"You are," I said. My hand came up to his cheek, thumb smoothing over the bone there. "You are doing right. If I want you to stop, I'll tell you."

"I know you will."

The truth of it settled deep in my chest. Although so much of him was wild, I knew he would never force me to do anything I wasn't ready for.

I tugged gently at the front of his shirt, pulling him closer. The kiss that followed wasn't careful anymore. It was still gentle, still patient, but there was a heat in it now that matched the pulse beating hard in my throat. His mouth moved against mine with barely contained primal need, learning the rhythm of my breathing, finding the places where I shivered, the edges of sounds I couldn't hold back.

The rest of the room faded out. The house. The Redneck Casanova. The world beyond the walls. There was only him, and his hand sliding down my waist. His palm covered most of my hip, fingers wrapping almost all the way around. The size of him hit me all over again, and I was admittedly intimidated.

"Jesus," I muttered against his mouth. "You are a lot of man."

He stilled. "Too much?"

Although I realized he may have been, I laughed, breathless. "Not in a bad way."

Relief moved through him, a slow exhale that ghosted across my lips. His thumb stroked my side in a hesitant little arc. He seemed to like the way my breath shuddered at that, because he did it again, a little surer this time.

Heat climbed my neck, setting me ablaze. The space between us felt charged—too soft, too close, too full of everything that had been building since the moment he stepped into my path in the forest and touched my cheek.

"Vek," I whispered, breath catching on the edge of his name. My lips were still warm from the kiss he'd given me moments before, and the space between us pulsed with the heat we weren't hiding anymore.

He didn't ask what I wanted. His mouth met mine again, slow at first, then deeper when I leaned into him. His hand tightened at my waist, his chest brushing mine in a way that carried both his strength and the effort it took not to take more.

I gripped his shirt, pulling him closer. "Come with me to the bedroom."

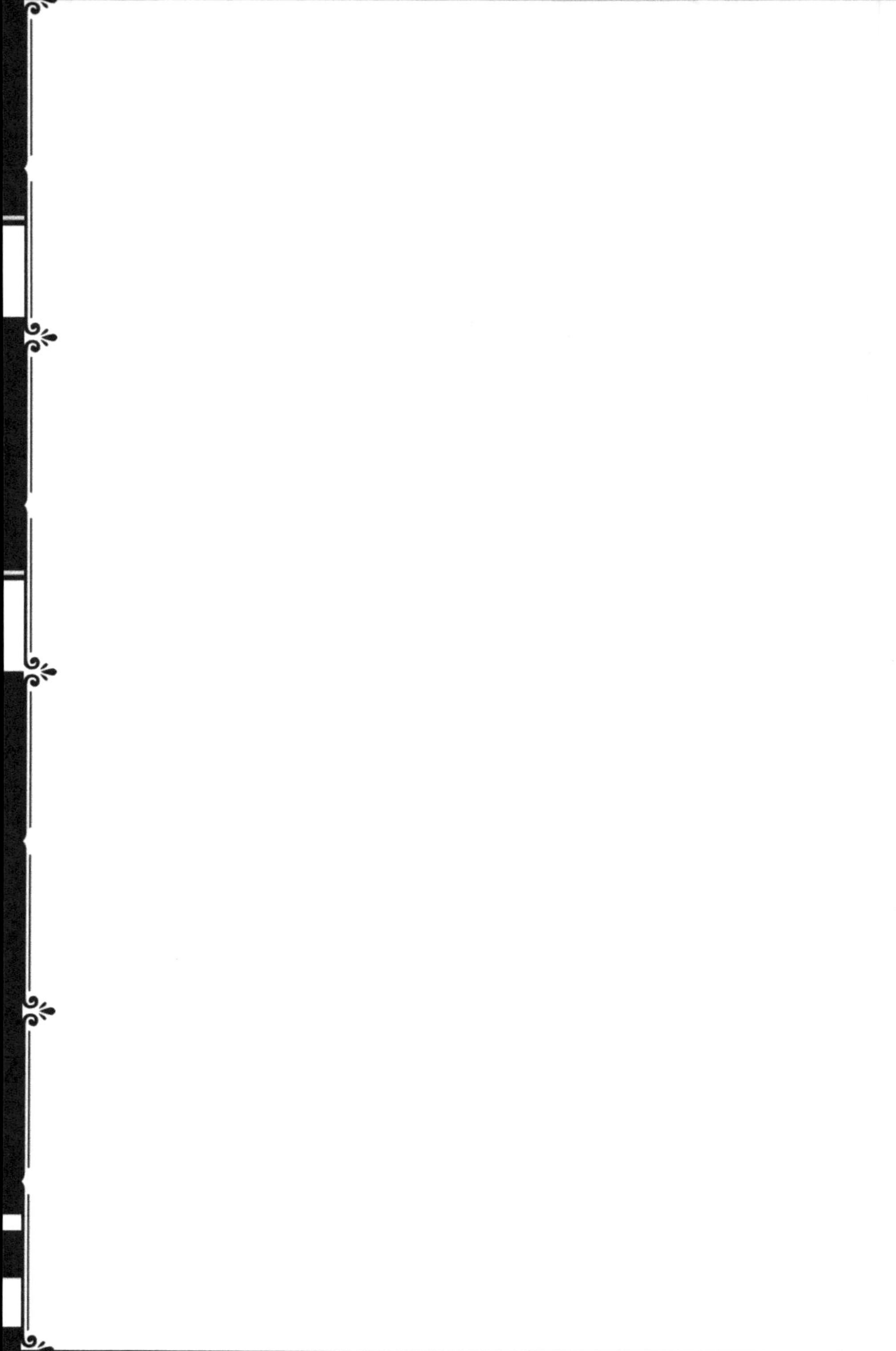

CHAPTER 11

Not Sorry

Olivia

Wasting no time, he lifted me, and the breath rushed out of me as my legs tightened around him. Every step toward the bedroom lit something deep inside me, the hallway turning into a blur of shadows and the soft scrape of his breath along my neck. My fingers tangled in his hair, trying to steady myself against the sudden rush of desire that left no space for thought.

My back met the doorframe for a heartbeat before he carried me into the bedroom. The faint glow from the lamp warmed the room, catching the tension in his face when he looked at me, and the heat in his eyes swept through me, sliding under my skin.

He lowered me onto the bed, the mattress dipping as his massive body followed. His hands traced up my thighs in a slow climb that stole the breath from my chest. Each inch he claimed sent a rush rolling through me, tightening everything at once. The air thickened with every breath we shared.

"If you want to stop..." I began, voice tight.

He pushed up onto his knees above me, his weight lifting from my hips, his brow tightening, his expression folding inward in a way that struck deeper than anything he could say. "You want me stop?"

The answer rushed out before I could think. "No." My next breath steadied it. "Not at all."

Some of the strain left his posture, and the shift in his eyes caught me off guard. He dipped his chin—a quiet nod—but the hesitation lingering there told me he was still bracing for another answer.

I knew he'd never been with a woman before, had never seen one like this, close enough to touch. Even so, my fingers trembled as I pulled my shirt over my head. Not from fear—because of him, because of the way he watched me, caught between wanting and not knowing how to reach for me.

His gaze moved over me in a slow sweep, and his breath hitched hard enough to hear. "Liv..."

I didn't look away as I dropped my bra on the floor. "You can touch me."

His hand lifted, hesitant at first, then surer when I didn't pull away. His fingers brushed beneath my ribs, tracing along my waist in a slow, exploring sweep. The touch sent a tight rush through my skin, a shiver sliding up my spine before I could stop it.

"Beautiful." He breathed it more than said it.

My hand rose on its own, brushing the hem of the shirt stretched across his chest. He pulled it over his head without looking away from me.

The sight of him—broad chest, copper fur, scars carved across muscle—sent a deep ache through me that left my breath unsteady.

When I pressed my palm to one of the pale marks, his heart leaped hard enough that I felt it against my wrist.

"This still hurts?" The question came out softer than I meant.

He gave a slow shake of his head. "Only memory."

Something shifted in his voice on that last word, something low and heavy. I leaned in and kissed the place just above the scar. His body shuddered under the touch, the reaction rolling through him before he pulled it back tight, holding himself in check for me.

My hand hooked behind his neck, guiding him down with me as I sank back onto the bed.

"You're not going to break anything," I murmured, my fingers tracing the warm line of his spine.

That pulled a soft, surprised sound from him.

He lowered himself over me, settling his weight until the press of him fit against every line of my body. His mouth found mine again, the kiss deepening until the room fell away.

A low sound escaped me when the feeling surged through my center, sharp enough to unravel whatever control I had left.

"Liv," he breathed into the kiss, voice rough with wanting.

I let my hands wander down his sides, following the lean lines of his body until my fingers slid beneath the loose waistband of his pants. The moment my palm closed around the hard thickness of him, he pulled in a harsh breath.

I didn't know how on God's green Earth he was going to fit that thing inside me, but I sure as hell was gonna let him try.

With my fingers hooked onto his waistband, I eased the fabric down over his hips. He helped, awkward only because the bed was small and there was so much of him. When the pants dropped to the floor, he looked at me like the world hinged on what I did next.

He was carved in shadow and lamplight—broad shoulders, long torso, strong thighs, fur and skin, and old scars that marked a life lived far from anyone who'd ever cared for him. He searched my face as if bracing for rejection.

Instead of flinching, I reached for him. My hand wrapped around the back of his thigh, drawing him closer with a confidence I didn't entirely feel but wanted him to believe.

"You're beautiful," I whispered.

The words barely formed before his breath broke, and whatever fear he'd been holding in his shoulders melted away.

He kissed me again—slower, deeper. His hand skimmed down my hip, fingers brushing the edge of my underwear before pausing. His eyes lifted, searching mine.

"This okay?" he asked quietly.

I needed him—every part of him—but he was being cautious with me. I wasn't sure I wanted him to be. "Yes." My voice trembled. "Please."

He tugged the fabric down my legs with a care that slowed everything around us. When his touch returned to my skin, it was gentle and exploratory, tracing my hip, my thigh—learning me—though his gaze never left my face.

When his fingers slipped between my legs and found where I ached, I gasped. My hips lifted toward him before I could stop them, and he froze instantly.

"Hurt?" he asked, pulling his hand back.

I grabbed his wrist and shook my head, trying to breathe. "No. God—no. It feels good."

He swallowed a thick, unsteady sound. "Show me."

So I did. Covering his much larger hand with mine, I guided him lower, adjusting his touch, letting him feel the way my body answered him.

"Here?" he murmured when he found my entrance, grazing my clit.

"Yes." My legs opened wider, nodding more of his touch than I needed air. "Right there."

When his big finger slid inside me, stretching me in all the best ways, my finger found its way to my clit, circling it exactly how I liked it. Heat coiled low and fast, winding my breath into ragged pieces. Each sound I made drew a deeper, rougher rumble from his chest, vibrating through me where his body brushed mine. The noises he pulled from me were obscene, and I nearly screamed when he added another finger.

"Liv," he whispered, awe tucked inside my name like he wasn't sure he was allowed to feel it.

"I'm okay," I managed, the words breaking. "Keep going. You're doing so good."

A quiet sound escaped him—soft, disbelieving, almost broken—but his fingers pushed deeper, giving me exactly what I needed. I reached for his cock with my other hand, using the slick at the tip to stroke him hard. His growl deepened, and his jaw flexed, but he didn't stop working me with his fingers. If anything, it urged him on.

The tension inside me tightened, and my hips ground against his hand without an ounce of shyness left in me. "Oh God. Vek." His name spilled out in a whine as I rolled against his fingers, chasing the climax that hovered just out of reach.

"I can smell..." His voice dropped into a growl I'd never heard before. Ignoring my groan of protest, he slid his fingers from inside me, leaving me aching and empty. He batted my hand away from my clit, then moved down my body, pushing my thighs as far apart as they would go before burying his face in my pussy.

Everything hit at once—tongue, nose, lips. He devoured me like he'd been starving for the taste, surrendering to every primal urge pulling him under. I couldn't stop him—I didn't want to. One hand dug into his hair for leverage while the other fisted in the blanket as I surged toward my orgasm.

"Don't stop, Vek." The words stumbled out, barely a shape. "Close. P-please."

The coil inside me drew tight—tighter—until the pressure snapped. My body arched into him as the orgasm tore through me, bursting stars behind my eyes. The sound that left me didn't feel human; it felt dragged up from somewhere deep.

Holding my thighs open, he followed me through it, kissing and sucking until I pushed weakly at his head.

When he finally pulled back, he stared at me in stunned stillness. Awe softened the hard lines of his face as he pressed gentle kisses to my thighs and stomach.

"Good?" he asked softly, adjusting his engorged cock as he moved up my body.

"So good," I breathed, completely spent.

His hand slid up to rest over my stomach, his expression softening. "I make you feel good?"

"Yes," I whispered. "You do."

Color rose beneath the fur on his cheeks, and he dipped his head as if he couldn't hold my gaze and my praise at once.

Curling my fingers into the hair at his nape, I pulled him down for a kiss, the taste of myself on his tongue making my pulse kick all over again.

"I want more," I murmured, my pussy clenching at the thought.

He swallowed hard. "I want..." His voice caught. "Don't want to hurt you."

"I know." My hand slipped between us and closed around the girth of him. The size stole a sharp breath from me. "We'll go slow. I'll be okay."

A low groan vibrated through him. His hips jerked in my hand before he forced himself still—muscles shaking with restraint.

"You tell me if hurts," he said, voice thick. "If you say stop, I stop."

"I know," I whispered. "And if I say more, you listen to that too."

A shaky smile tugged at his mouth. "I listen."

And the way he said it sent a pulse of heat through my core.

Kissing me again, Vek lowered himself between my thighs with a care that might've made me smile if the moment hadn't been wound so tight. His hands slid beneath my knees, guiding my legs around his hips. The size difference became impossible to ignore—his body fitting against mine in a way that felt overwhelming and right all at once.

A whisper slipped out before I could stop it. "Lord... this is gonna be a lot."

He stilled. "Too much?"

"No," I said, smoothing my hand over his chest. "Not too much. Just... a lot." My voice shook. "I want you. All of you. We'll go slow."

Something inside him loosened. His breath shivered through him, and he dipped his forehead toward mine even though I was too short for him to reach. "Okay."

He guided himself toward me, one hand braced near my head as if shielding me from more than just his weight. The first press of him nudged at my entrance, a slow bloom of pressure where our bodies met. The whole room seemed to hold still.

There was pressure. Stretch. A deep, steady ache that wasn't pain—just the shock of so much man fitting into so little space.

My fingers curled into his ribcage, and he went rigid above me.

"Liv?" His voice rasped, frayed at the edges. "Hurt?"

"It's… intense," I whispered, shaking my head. "But good. I just need a second."

He nodded, and the tremor running through his arms shook the bed frame. "I wait."

Every part of him went perfectly still—muscles locked, breaths careful, like he feared even shifting wrong might break me. I eased my hips the slightest bit, letting my body find the angle it needed, giving myself a moment to adjust.

"Okay," I breathed. "More."

With more control than I thought possible, he pushed in slowly—inch by agonizing inch. A soft burn warmed into heat, spreading low and deep, drawing a helpless sound from my throat.

By the time he was fully seated inside me, sweat shimmered along his temples. His breathing had turned uneven, chest rising in long, strained pulls.

"Liv..." His voice fractured. "You feel..."

"Good?" I asked softly.

His answer wasn't a word—just a sound torn from somewhere deep. "Yes. Good. Too good."

A breathless laugh escaped me. "That's the idea."

Curling over me, his mouth found mine again, kissing away every flicker of uncertainty, every trace of tension. The first roll of his hips was barely a movement, just enough to let my body settle around the fullness of him. The second drew a muted gasp from my throat. The third unspooled something inside both of us.

He listened with his whole body.

The shift of my breath. The arch of my spine. The soft sounds slipping out no matter how I tried to hold them in.

Every time I reacted, he followed—testing, learning, adjusting with a tenderness that shouldn't have fit the sheer strength of him. His gaze moved between my mouth and my eyes, watching every change in my face as if it showed him where to go next.

"You're following me," I whispered, wonder edging each word.

His breath brushed my cheek. "Yes. I follow you."

The rhythm sank deeper—still controlled, still slow, but carrying a new weight. Something tight coiled inside me again, building fast, fed by the way he breathed my name against my temple, unable to hold it in.

"Liv..." His voice cracked. "I feel... so much. I don't want to hurt. I don't want to stop."

"You're not hurting me." I lifted my hips into him, seeking more. "You're perfect. Keep going. *Please*."

The plea tugged something loose inside him.

His next thrust found a deeper angle, and the world burst behind my eyelids. A broken sound tore from me—half gasp, half release—and he answered with a low, gutted noise that vibrated through every point where our bodies met.

Everything narrowed to the steady, building drive of his hips. The creak of the mattress. The slick heat between us. Spring air clinging to sweat and skin.

My legs tightened around him. His breath caught, hips driving harder, deeper, searching. The pressure climbed fast—rising, relentless—and then I shattered. A scream ripped out of me as my orgasm crashed through every nerve, fiercer than the first.

"Liv..." he moaned, voice frayed with desperation. "I'm... close. I can't..."

"Yes," I panted, my body still twitching through the aftershocks. Each slow roll of his hips drew it out again. "It's okay. I've got you. Let go."

His whole body jolted, fighting the instinct to stay in control even now. One more careful stroke. Then another.

And the wave broke.

He buried his face against my temple as release slammed through him. A roar ripped from his chest, deep enough to shake the headboard, but he still held himself above me with trembling arms, terrified of crushing me even as pleasure wracked him in hard, shuddering pulses.

The feel of him losing control inside that much restraint tipped me straight over the edge again. Heat detonated inside me, spilling outward in bright, dizzying waves. My fingers dug into his back, gripping fur and slick skin and the staggering strength of him as my climax rolled through me a third time.

When the aftershocks eased, Vek shifted just enough to take some of his weight off me—still inside, still careful, still watching my face as though reading the aftermath as closely as he'd read the moment itself. His hand found mine where it trembled against the sheet. Long fingers threaded through my own, anchoring me with a warmth that softened every last shiver.

"You safe?" he asked, voice rubbed raw.

"With you?" My thumb traced along his knuckles. "Yeah. I am."

The breath he let out held relief, tangled with something he didn't yet have words for. He slipped free with slow gentleness, then guided me onto my side and followed a heartbeat later. My back settled to his chest as though he'd been built for this, one strong arm circling my waist and drawing me into his heat.

Every muscle in my body hummed—loose, spent, satisfied in ways I wasn't sure I'd ever felt before. Something in my chest loosened and then opened quietly inside me, a tender ache I wasn't brave enough to name.

He nuzzled into my hair, inhaling lightly, as if memorizing the scent of us—shampoo, sweat, spring, something new that belonged only to this room. "Good," he murmured against my neck. "You with me. Good."

The words weren't perfect. They didn't have to be.

At the foot of the bed, Boone let out a long, theatrical sigh—the canine equivalent of signing off on the situation. June Bug startled awake, blinked blearily at us as though we'd disrupted her favorite nest, then tucked herself back into her pile of laundry.

Thunder had rolled off into the ridge, leaving the house wrapped in a gentler kind of quiet. Sleep tugged at my vision, coaxing me toward it.

This didn't feel like temptation winning or common sense losing. It didn't feel reckless, or borrowed, or foolish. It felt like an opening. Like stepping through the first door of something I'd spent years circling without realizing it.

His hand settled over my stomach again, and my fingers curled over his without thinking.

"Vek?" The word drifted out of me, blurred by sleep.

"Yes?" His voice brushed my ear, softer than I'd ever heard it.

"I'm not sorry," I whispered.

A long breath filled his chest behind me, warming my back. "Not sorry, too," he murmured, quiet as a secret meant for the dark.

The night settled into peace around us—the beams, the mountain—everything calm for the first time in a long time.

Wrapped in the arms of a man the world insisted didn't exist, I let my eyes close. Loneliness, that old familiar ache, slipped away so easily it startled me.

For once, I wasn't alone at all.

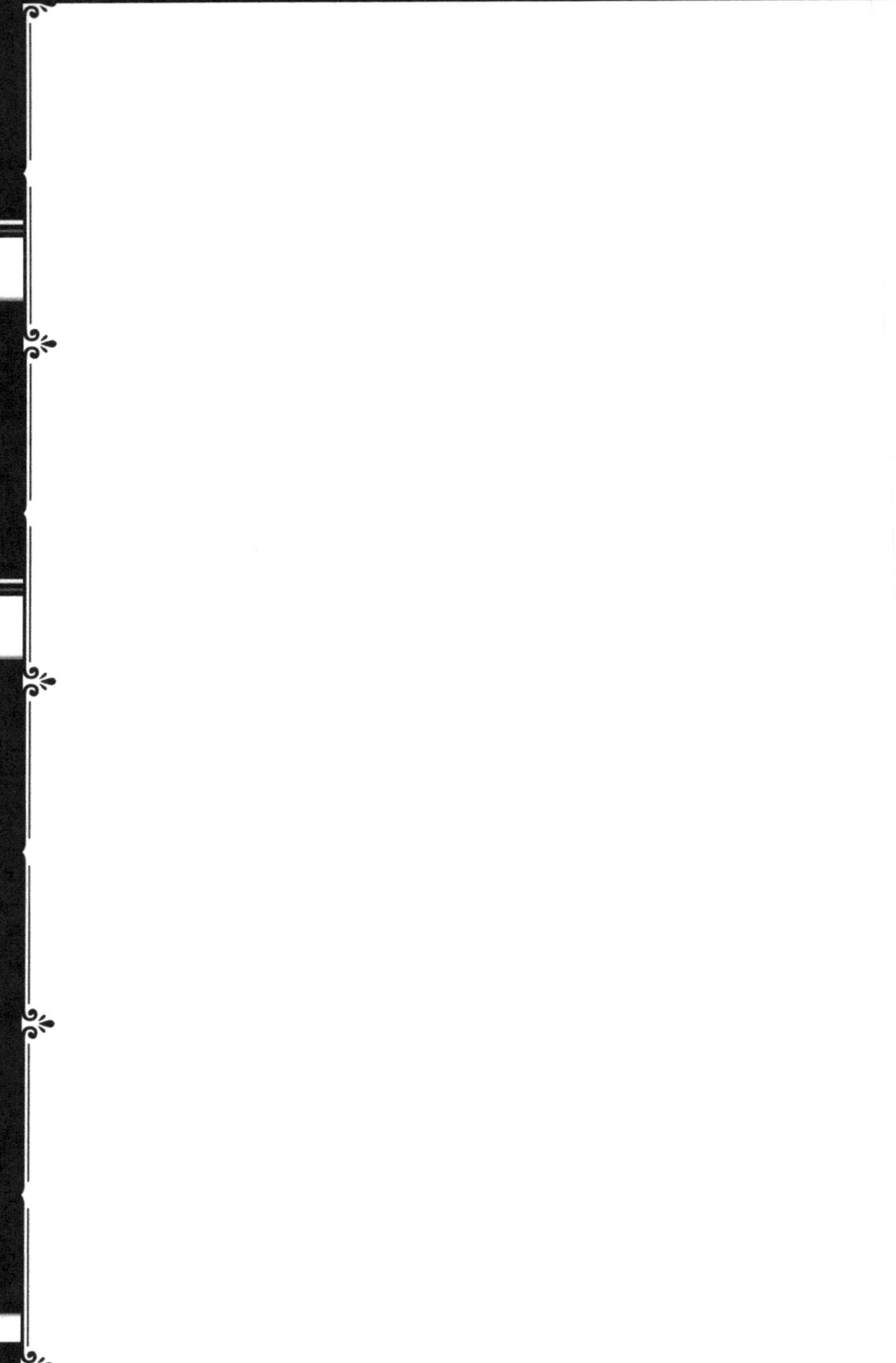

CHAPTER 12

Trouble Before Breakfast

Olivia

Sunlight crept into the bedroom, warming its way across the quilt before finding the curve of Vek's shoulder and finally brushing my skin. The heat pulled a breath out of me before my mind caught up.

Then my body reminded me what we'd done.

A tender pull settled deep in my thighs, another ache low in my belly. The memory hit with enough force to make me bury my face in the pillow.

"Lord have mercy," I muttered, my voice rasping like it had been used too well.

Vek lay beside me in an easy sprawl, turned toward me without meaning to. One arm above his head, the other across his chest. Peace softened his features—something I'd never seen when he was awake and bracing for danger. His chest rose and fell in a slow rhythm. June Bug had her belly pressed against his ribs. Boone guarded my robe like he'd been sworn in as security.

Lavender clung to the sheets, mingled with the faint warmth we'd poured into them hours ago.

My hips protested when I shifted, sharp enough that a sound slipped out before I could stop it.

The peaceful set of his face shifted at once—instinct waking before the rest of him. His hand reached across the quilt, searching for me even though his eyes were still closed.

June Bug grumbled, abandoned her post, and flopped onto the floor. Sunlight hit Vek's jaw as he shifted, washing warm over the soft fur there.

For a moment, I just let myself look at him.

The faint parting of his lips. The dark sweep of his fur, messy from sleep. People would call him a monster, but here, with the morning resting on his skin, he looked more human than most men ever bothered to be.

He moved closer. His knee brushed mine beneath the quilt, and a warm spark traveled straight through me. The ache softened into something else. Something bold enough to speed my heart.

His eyes opened slowly, the morning pulling him awake in slow pieces. When his gaze found mine, he seemed to relax.

"Liv," he murmured, voice rough with sleep.

The way he said my name loosened something deep in my chest. "Morning," I whispered.

A small, sleepy smile tugged at his mouth. "Morning."

I tried to sit, but my hips made their displeasure known. A hiss escaped before I could swallow it.

In a heartbeat, he was propped on one elbow, fully awake, eyes sharp with worry. "Hurt?"

"Not hurt," I rushed out. "Just sore."

He took that in, his brow tightening in a way that carried concern and something warmer beneath it. "From me?"

Heat crawled up my neck. "Yes. And don't look proud."

He tried to hide the smile, but it still showed at the corner of his mouth. "I was gentle."

"You were. But there's only so gentle you can be when you're..." my hand waved at all of him "...you."

That did something to him. Not smugness—*heat*. His body kicked up its own warmth. He moved closer, his hand slipping beneath the quilt until his palm found my waist. His thumb stroked the skin there, slow enough to make my breath catch.

The ache changed instantly. Desire worked its way up through the soreness like it had only been waiting for a touch.

As though he felt the change, his gaze deepened, need flaring in his golden irises.

"You need rest," he murmured, though the stroke of his thumb told a different story.

"I don't want rest."

Whatever held him still released at once.

He leaned in until our foreheads touched. "You ache."

"Yes," I whispered. "But not in a way that wants space."

Breath leaving in one quiet exhale, he slid his hand down the curve of my thigh beneath the quilt.

"More?"

A shiver ran through me. "Not fast," I said softly. "But yes."

He moved before the words even finished leaving my mouth, the mattress dipping beneath his weight. The air between us thickened, charged with wanting.

He kissed me, coaxing me awake all over again. When I tugged him closer, the kiss deepened, heat blooming in my stomach.

"Olivia," he murmured against my mouth, the sound thick and warm.

My fingers curled in his fur. "Come here."

He eased over me with the same care he'd given me last night, bracing himself so his weight didn't crush me. His chest brushed mine, fur warm against bare skin. His mouth traveled down my throat, then closed gently around my nipple. I arched into him, breath breaking.

A quiet rumble vibrated through his chest. He nudged forward again, letting himself stroke through the wetness in long, steady passes that made my thighs tighten around him.

"You feel ready," he murmured in my ear.

"I am. I want you."

When he kissed me again, the kind of kiss that stole thought, his hips shifted, guiding the head of his cock to my entrance.

The first push stretched me open, Heat flooded my belly as I dragged my nails lightly along his shoulders. "More. All of you."

"Liv…" His voice broke, raw. "You feel—"

Words failed him.

He groaned, the sound coming from somewhere primal. He pushed deeper, slow enough that my body had time to take him. When he sank fully inside, we both stilled, breath tangled in the space between us.

"Tell me if hurts," he whispered.

"I'll tell you," I murmured. "Move."

With a nod, he drew back just enough to make me gasp, then pushed in again with a long, steady stroke. Each movement found the places inside me that had woken hungry for him.

I lifted my hips to meet him. "Just like that," I breathed. "Don't stop."

His mouth found mine again and his hand cupped my breast, thumb circling the peak until soft sounds spilled from me without thought.

Pleasure built fast, impossible to hold back.

"Vek..." My voice wavered. "I'm close."

Curling down, his forehead pressed to mine. "Good."

The next thrust sent the world peeling open. Pleasure swept through me in a deep wave. My back arched, fingers tightening in his fur.

He shuddered, his voice catching. "Liv—"

Thrusting a few more times, his breath broke, then heat spilled deep inside me as his body shook above mine. He held himself up, still protecting me even when everything in him burst apart.

When the tremors faded, he settled onto his side and hauled me with him like I weighed nothing. His arm wrapped around my waist, his hand warm at my back, his chest a solid wall of heat that made my eyelids droop all over again.

"We should get up," I whispered—mostly for my own conscience.

"Mmm," he hummed into my hair, which was not an answer but also absolutely an answer.

I knew I should've been worrying about breakfast, or laundry, or the fact that the universe still expected me to function like a normal adult. Instead, all I could feel was the warmth of him against me and the steady pull of his breathing.

So I let my eyes close. Let the morning wait. Let myself sink back into him.

Because somehow, in the span of one impossible night, I'd ended up curled against a man the world would call a monster... and all I felt was safe. And already in far more trouble than I'd planned for.

I woke again to Boone's low rumble drifting through the room. It wasn't loud, but it carried a note he didn't use unless someone pulled into the driveway. I blinked against the soft light and pushed up onto an elbow, the quilt sliding from my waist.

Beside me, Vek stirred. His brow knit as he lifted his head, already alert in a way that made my pulse jump.

An unmistakable knock followed, but not the aggressive one from the night before.

"Liv?" Gunner called from the porch. "You home?"

My stomach dropped straight through the mattress.

"Oh, hell," I whispered, scrambling upright. The ache from earlier flared again, sharp enough to steal my breath. I grabbed the quilt and pulled it against me, my mind racing faster than my hands could keep up.

Vek sat up fully now, eyes shifting between me and the door. "Liv?" he murmured, uncertainty filling his gaze.

"It's my brother," I said under my breath. "Just... stay in here. *Please*."

He didn't understand all of it, the risk of him being seen, but he understood enough. His jaw remained tense, but he sank back onto the bed, watchful but waiting.

Another knock, harder this time.

"Liv! I know you're home!"

"Coming!" I called, trying to make it sound normal even though nothing about this moment felt remotely normal.

Reaching for my robe, I cinched it tight, and ran a hand through my hair, hoping it made a difference. June Bug and Boone swarmed my ankles, which didn't help my composure one bit.

I gave Vek one last look. "Stay."

He nodded, a quiet assurance in his eyes that told me he would stay where I needed him. Or at least, I hoped he would.

Blowing out a breath, I shut the door behind me and headed down the hall with a heart that felt one beat away from launching itself out of my chest.

I opened the front door and tried for something close to casual. "Morning," I said, though my voice barely cooperated. Both dogs darted past, breaking the tension for a moment.

Gunner stood on the porch holding two cups of coffee, looking entirely too awake for the hour. His jeans were damp from wet grass, and the wind had worked his hair into a mess he hadn't bothered to fix.

"Finally," he said, handing me one of the cups. "I was just about to grab my key."

"Sorry, I stayed up too late," I replied, taking a sip of the coffee. It was true enough. Just not in the way he'd imagine.

Something in the way he studied my face made me want to pull the robe tighter around me. He'd always been too good at reading between lines, picking up on things before I said them out loud. The curse of being so close.

"You look... flushed," he said, squinting at me.

"It's warm inside," I blurted, immediately regretting my choice of words.

Gunner lifted an eyebrow. Not accusing—just curious in the worst possible way. He knew something was up, and I was a terrible liar.

"Anyway," he said, shaking his head a little, "I came by because I wanted to talk to you face-to-face."

My stomach tightened. "About what?"

"T-Bone," he said, voice dropping, as if the name itself carried trouble.

Of course. Of all mornings for this conversation.

"He's been out at The Rusty Spur mouthing off again," Gunner continued. "Saying he saw something big on your property the other night. Something worth bragging about."

My throat dried. "He's still going on about that?" I hadn't told Gunner about T-Bone's intrusion the night before, and I wasn't sure I wanted to.

"Still?" Gunner huffed. "Liv, he's got half the boys at the bar ready to come out here. Talking about hunting, tracking—hell, you know how stupid they get when they've had a few. He's making it into a damn event."

A cold ripple moved through my chest. "You think he'll actually show up?"

"I don't know," he admitted. "I warned him to stay away, but I didn't want you blindsided if he didn't listen."

He shifted his weight on the porch step, looking past me again, scanning the house like he expected trouble inside it too.

"I didn't plan on coming out here today, but...I guess I wanted to check on you. Make sure you're okay."

I forced a small laugh. "I'm fine. Just didn't sleep enough. And Boone barking woke me up fast."

"Mm-hm," he said, not convinced. "You're acting... jumpy."

Stepping back a little, he rubbed the back of his neck. "Listen. Please keep the doors locked today. Don't go wandering around the property at night alone, okay? If T-Bone and his buddies are half as loud as Riggs said they were last night, you'll hear 'em before they're on the drive."

"I won't" I said, softer than I meant. I didn't like not having freedom to walk around my own property, but I didn't want to put Vek at risk. Eventually, T-Bone would move on to something else. I hoped.

Gunner gave me a long look—the kind he used when we were kids and he sensed something was wrong even before I said a word. His voice gentled. "If anything feels off, call me."

"I promise."

I thought Gunner would turn away and leave then, but Boone darted back inside, barking, and Gunner's eyes followed the sound past my shoulder.

"What's gotten into him?" he asked.

Before I could answer, June Bug darted past me as well, nails scattering across the hardwood like she'd remembered something important. Boone followed her, both dogs alert and laser-focused on the bedroom door.

Gunner's brows pulled together. "Liv... what's going on?"

"Nothing, I—wait—Gunner—"

But he was already stepping inside.

"Hold on—" I grabbed his arm, but he moved past me with the kind of stubborn momentum that ran through our bloodline.

He rounded the corner and stopped dead.

Vek stood at the end of the hallway.

He wasn't hiding. He wasn't threatening. He simply was—tall, bare-chested, bandage around his arm, fur tousled from sleep. His posture stayed even, his gaze flicking between Gunner and me, waiting for direction.

Boone barked once. June Bug trotted straight up to him and sat at his feet.

Gunner didn't breathe for a full second. "Liv," he whispered, "what am I looking at?"

Stepping forward, I placed myself where both could see me. "His name is Vek."

Gunner's hand drifted toward his belt. I lifted my palm sharply. "Don't. You'll scare him."

Gunner froze, swallowing hard as he stared at Vek. "That's him, isn't it? The one you saw. The one T-Bone's been running his mouth about."

"And the one I shot," I said quietly. "The one who didn't raise a hand to me. The one I brought into my barn because he was bleeding and alone."

Vek stayed still, watching my face.

Gunner's jaw worked as he tried to make sense of what he was seeing. "He's... big," he said finally.

"I'm aware," I muttered.

Taking one slow step forward, Vek lowered his head just slightly—a gesture that felt more re-spectful than submissive. His gaze moved be-tween us, then settled on Gunner.

"Gunner," he said, the word rough but recogniz-able.

Gunner flinched. "He talks?"

"Better than I expected," I said. "He understands far more."

Gunner blinked hard, absorbing that. Knowing him as well as I did, I could see the moment he realized panic wouldn't help.

Clearing his throat, he took a sip of his coffee. "He's not safe here with T-Bone riling up people in town. He's got a handful of drunk, eager idiots happy to follow him into any shenanigans he's willing to lead them into."

My pulse stumbled. "I'm not sending him away."

Gunner nodded, but his jaw flexed. "I don't know what to tell you, Liv. Those boys aren't careful. They'll shoot at anything that looks like a shadow, and with him here, you're in danger too."

Vek's attention snapped toward the mention of shooting. Gunner noticed.

"Liv," Gunner continued, "if they come here and see him..." He exhaled sharply. "They won't ask questions. They won't think. They'll fire."

"I know," I whispered.

Gunner turned to Vek, worry etched plainly across his face. "You protect her?"

Vek nodded once, no hesitation. "Yes."

The word hit like a promise.

With a hard swallow, Gunner nodded back. "Then I'm trusting both of you. But if anything feels wrong—anything—you call me. Immediately."

"I will."

He took one last look at Vek, equal parts cautious and respectful, then returned to the porch. Before stepping outside, he pressed a hand to my shoulder.

"And Liv?" he said quietly.

"Yeah?"

"Try not to piss T-Bone off. He ain't got any sense. Just stay out of his way."

Dread burned up my throat, but I forced a laugh. "I'll keep that in mind."

CHAPTER 13

The Ridge and the Reckoning

Olivia

By the following day, a strange quiet settled into the house. I'd made three laps around the living room before I realized afternoon had slipped in without changing a damn thing about the unease in my chest. Boone followed every pass with the focus of a man watching a tennis match. June Bug bounced between us, her nails tapping out the same restless rhythm running through my muscles.

Vek stood near the window, body angled toward the ridge, shoulders relaxed but alert all the same. He didn't lift the curtain or shift his stance — just listened the way he did when something outside nudged at instincts older than mine.

"You walk since morning," he said quietly.

"Feels better than sitting," I muttered, rubbing warmth into my arms. "Last night was quiet. Too quiet. So now my brain thinks there's a reason for it."

His ear tipped slightly. "You feel something."

"Apparently." I sighed. "Wish I didn't."

A look through the blinds offered the same view I'd grown up with, though it didn't ease the tightness in my chest the way it should have. The trees held steady in the sun-warmed air, the ridge calm, the yard exactly as it had always been.

Boone didn't buy it. Pushing to his feet, he shifted his weight forward, ears locked toward the backyard. June Bug went rigid beside him before pressing into my leg like she wanted to climb straight up it.

"Okay," I whispered, "that's new."

Vek's attention sharpened. It wasn't dramatic—just a subtle tightening in the line of his back, a shift that told me he picked up something too. "Dogs smell early."

"That's what I was afraid of."

My rifle leaned in the corner beside the bookshelf, exactly where I'd set it after Gunner left. I wasn't ready to touch it, but knowing it wasn't far kept my pulse from tipping into panic.

Without a sound, Vek stepped behind me. The warmth of his hand settled low on my back, steady and reassuring in a way that loosened some of the tension coiled beneath my ribs.

"You call brother?" he asked.

"Not unless I need to." I tried for a steady breath. "He's already back in the city. He'll come if I ask, but it'll take him time."

Vek nodded once. "He come when you say."

"Yeah," I said softly. "Just... not fast."

Boone let out a deeper huff, the one that never came without reason. June Bug trembled against my shin, tiny body vibrating with unspent alarm. Leaning over, I picked her up, tucking her against my chest and petting her gently.

Vek listened again, head tilting. "Air different."

A tight breath escaped me. "I hate how you phrase things sometimes."

He didn't answer, which only confirmed my suspicion that he noticed something subtle I couldn't see yet.

Still, the ridge stayed still. The house stayed quiet. My heartbeat didn't follow suit.

"Maybe Gunner wasn't overreacting," I murmured. But I knew, even if I couldn't yet see anything outside, that I was lying.

Evening crept into the house in a slow drift, softening the edges of the furniture and washing the walls in a dim amber glow. It should've been comforting, but it wasn't. Something taut lived under the quiet, hanging on no matter how the hours slipped by.

Boone settled beneath the table near Vek's legs, planted firm like he meant to hold the room together by sheer will. June Bug perched on the arm of the sofa, every nerve in her body aimed toward the window, unusually still for her size and temperament.

Vek stood near the front room again, shoulders tighter than they'd been at midday, gaze fixed on the treeline. His breath had taken on a quieter rhythm—the kind he used when he was listening to things I couldn't hear.

"What is it?" I whispered.

He lifted his chin slightly. "Wind gone."

I listened. The trees outside held perfectly still. No rustle of leaves. No chatter from the branches. Even the insects had quieted, leaving the atmosphere too thick for a normal spring evening.

The silence in the house sharpened every sound—the hum of the refrigerator, the tick of the clock, even my own heartbeat pressing hard against my ribs.

Vek inhaled, glancing through the curtains. "They close."

My pulse leapt. "Who?"

His gaze shifted toward the left side of the property. Boone rose at the same instant, a deep growl climbing through his chest. When I stepped toward the window, Vek's hand closed gently around my wrist and pulled me back a pace.

"Stay behind."

Something in the air shifted. A faint vibration moved through the floorboards—so slight I never would've caught it on my own. The hair along my arms lifted.

Vek listened with a focus that made the room feel smaller. "Engines," he murmured. "Coming fast."

The dread hit me hard, twisting my stomach until I thought I might be sick.

ATVs. Trucks. Tires grinding through mud and gravel. More than a few.

"Oh God... *please*, not today."

Moving in front of me, Vek stood against the door. "Call brother."

My fingers stumbled for the phone. To my relief, Gunner answered immediately.

"Liv?"

"They're here," I said, voice shaking. "T-Bone brought a group. Six... maybe more."

"I'm coming," he said. "Half an hour out. Keep your lights down and stay away from the windows."

"Just hurry," I whispered.

"I will."

The call dropped, and my breath wavered, tears threatening to fall. For a moment, I thought about calling the cops, but I couldn't. Not with Vek in my home. I couldn't risk his safety even more.

Vek touched my shoulder, pulling me out of my panic. "He come."

"Too far," I murmured.

The engines swelled as they cut across the ridge, each rev sharper than the last. Boone planted himself at the front door beside Vek, barking with a ferocity I'd never heard from him. June Bug pressed into my leg, trembling so hard her tiny body vibrated against my calf. Needing to calm myself as much as her, I picked her up and held her close.

Headlights broke through the trees in harsh beams. One ATV hit the dip in the drive. Then another. Then a third. Two trucks followed, weaving in drunken, uneven arcs.

A sharp pain tightened under my ribs. "Come on, Gunner. *Hurry.*"

The men spilled out like they'd been rehearsing it. T-Bone led them, swagger sloppy, beer bottle dangling from his hand. The others fanned out behind him with flashlights, pipes, boards—anything that felt like a weapon to men with too much alcohol and too little sense.

Vek pulled me into a quick hug before bracing his back against the door. Boone's barking echoed through the house, June Bug adding her frenzied trill to the chaos.

Shouts hit the yard in jagged bursts.

"Come out!"

"We know it's in there!"

"Bring it out!"

My breath thinned. "This is starting."

Vek didn't take his eyes off the yard. "Doors locked?"

"All of them."

Flashlights swept across the siding. The group began spreading out across the lawn, moving in wide circles, voices sharp with liquid courage.

"They're surrounding us," I said quietly, though my heart beat in a frantic rhythm.

"We stay together," he replied. "Get gun."

Setting June Bug down, I reached for my rifle and cocked it, hoping I wouldn't have to take a shot at someone again.

A heavy fist struck the side of the house with enough force to rattle the windowpanes. Laughter followed. Another blow landed from farther back.

T-Bone bellowed above the rest, voice thick with booze. "Show yourself, big man!"

Boone lunged harder, barking until he nearly scraped through the frame. June Bug darted beneath a chair, shaking uncontrollably.

My phone buzzed with Gunner's message:

Fifteen minutes out. Don't move.

Fifteen minutes might as well have been a lifetime.

Footsteps thudded across the porch. Several sets. Someone tugged hard on the doorknob. Another cursed with frustration. A third slammed a shoulder into the door, making the chair beneath the knob jump.

Vek adjusted his stance, coverage widening, body bracing.

"They try break in," he said.

I nodded, leaning to the side to peek through the curtain. "They're getting close."

The next blow struck harder—a deep, jarring impact that cracked the frame near the hinge and caused me to stumble back. Boone barked so fiercely the door shook behind him.

Shadows crossed the small pane near the top of the door, flashlight beams jittering in broken paths.

"Get off my porch!" My voice tore from me without thought. "Or I'll shoot!"

The words didn't even slow them.

The next slam hit like a sledgehammer. The top panel split. A wild laugh cracked through the dark. Then a fist punched through the small square window beside the door, sending glass across the floor in a glittering spray.

I screamed as an arm shoved through the opening, reaching blindly for the lock.

"Back!" I kicked his arm hard enough that he lost balance and pulled away. A man cursed outside, another shoved past him. "I swear to God I'll shoot your damn arm off if you stick it back in my house!"

"Break it!"

"Push through!"

"Move!"

The door heaved again. Vek threw his weight forward, holding the door with all his strength. June Bug whimpered beneath my leg.

Then someone lost patience entirely.

"Shoot it!"

Time paused—just long enough for terror to anchor itself in my bones.

The gunshot shattered the window to the right of the door, spraying the room with shards of glass. Boone howled. June Bug flattened herself to the boards.

Vek jerked back from the impact.

A thin, stunned sound slipped out of him—more breath than voice. Red droplets hit the floorboards in quick, startling spatters.

"No—Vek—" I caught him as his knees buckled, but he slipped from my grasp, crashing against the floorboards as if his strength had failed him all at once.

"Vek!" My voice broke as I dropped beside him, hands shaking so violently I could barely see.

Blood warmed my palms. His breath stuttered.

Outside, the men shouted as several truck engines entered the fray from down the drive. *Gunner.*

Boots hit the ground. Something slammed into the house again. The world narrowed to the man bleeding at my feet while the yard erupted outside.

"Stay with me," I begged, voice cracking. "*Please*—stay with me..."

His breath faltered again.

And everything inside me went cold.

The Night I Almost Lost Him

Olivia

Blood soaked through my fingers faster than I could stem it, warm and slick against my palms as I pressed harder into the torn flesh along Vek's ribs. My breath came in sharp, shallow bursts, but

I kept forcing it steady, forcing myself to stay with him.

"Vek—look at me," I whispered, leaning over him as he fought to keep his eyes open. "Hey. Stay here."

His gaze wavered, unfocused at first, then locked on my face like he needed me to hold him here.

"Hurts," he rasped.

"I know, baby, I know." My hands trembled against the wound. "Hold on. *Please*—hold on."

June Bug pressed against my thigh, trembling so hard her whole body shook the floorboards beneath us. Boone stood over both of them, bristled and rumbling in a low, exhausted growl as he kept one eye on the broken window.

Vek drew in a ragged breath and flinched when fresh blood welled between my fingers. Yanking off my jacket, I pressed it as hard as I could against the wound. "Liv..." The sound of my name broke something in me, the tears falling without my permission.

"Stay with me," I whispered, my forehead hovering just above his. "I've got you. Just breathe. I'm not losing you tonight."

His expression softened, even through the pain. "Scared... for you."

That undid me. I shook my head, tears blurring the floorboards beneath us. "Don't worry about me—*God*, Vek, you can't—you don't get to worry about me when you're lying here bleeding."

The words hitched in my throat before I could stop them. "I can't lose you. I love you." It spilled out raw and bare, more truth than confession, too late to take back and too urgent to swallow.

Even though he was in pain, something eased in his face.

"You love," he murmured, the syllables barely holding together. "Me?"

"Yes," I breathed. "Yes, I do. So you stay with me, do you hear me? *Stay.*"

His hand twitched against the floor, trying to find mine. I caught it immediately, palm to palm, blood and sweat mixing between our fingers as I returned it to press the wound with my other.

Outside, engines revved and tires skidded across gravel—trucks pulling up fast, but none of the chaos reached him. His focus stayed locked on me—on my voice, on the pressure I kept against the wound.

"Liv," he whispered again, weaker than before.

"Right here." I pressed my forehead gently to his, keeping my voice steady even as fear clawed up my spine. "I'm right here, Vek. You're not alone. Just—just keep breathing. That's all you have to do."

His chest rose unevenly against my arm. "Stay...?"

"Yes," I said. "I'm staying. As long as it takes."

Heavy boots hit the porch fast, the boards trembling under the weight of men rushing toward the broken door. Boone barked until his voice cracked, but I couldn't look away from Vek. My hands stayed locked to the wound, heat and blood and panic all sliding together beneath my palms.

The front door shoved inward, catching on the cracked hinge. Mason squeezed through first, eyes sweeping the foyer before he froze hard.

"Gunner—here!" he shouted back over his shoulder, voice breaking. "He's down—he's bleeding—"

Gunner barreled through the doorway a heartbeat later. The second he saw the floor—saw Vek, saw my hands soaked red—he dropped to his knees so fast the impact rattled the boards.

"Christ—Liv—he's hit." His voice cracked. "Riggs! Get your med bag—now!"

Riggs, still outside on the porch, leaned in behind them. His eyes went wide at the sight of the blood, shock cutting a full second off his reaction before instinct shoved him into motion.

"On it," he said, turning on his heel and sprinting back toward his truck.

I kept my hands pressed to Vek's side, refusing to give the blood any more ground. "Help's coming," I whispered, voice shaking. "Stay awake. *Please*."

Vek's fingers squeezed my hand. "Stay... with Liv."

"Yes," I said. "With me. I've got you."

A moment later, Riggs rushed back through the doorway, a medical bag slung over his shoulder and breath coming fast. He dropped to the floor across from me without wasting a beat.

Let me in,' he said, voice steady now, dropping straight into the work. "Liv—don't move your hands yet."

"I'm not," I whispered, scooting over just enough to give him space.

Riggs brushed blood aside with careful fingers, leaning in to get a better look. His jaw tightened. "High shot. That's something. We can work with that."

Gunner hovered just behind him, shaking but steadying himself by sheer force. "Tell me what you need."

"Towels, light," Riggs said. "We clean it before anything else."

Mason moved immediately, sprinting toward the kitchen. Gunner scraped a lamp from the side table and dragged it closer, angling the light down toward the wound.

"Liv," Riggs said softly, "I'm going to need you to lift your hand in a minute—but only when I say."

Fear clenched tight in my chest. "Just tell me when."

He met my eyes briefly, grounding the moment in something calm and human before leaning back toward Vek.

"Hang on, big guy," Riggs murmured. "We're gonna take care of you."

Mason hurried back into the room with an armful of towels and dropped to his knees beside Gunner. The first clean towel hit Riggs's outstretched hand before Mason even caught his breath.

"Good," Riggs muttered, sliding the folded cloth under my elbow. "Liv—on three."

I braced myself, hands shaking so badly I worried I'd lose my grip before he reached "two."

"One... two... *three.*"

I lifted my hand a few inches—no more—and fresh blood spilled over Riggs's wrist in a sudden, terrifying bloom.

A sound broke out of me, half sob, half prayer.

"It's okay," Riggs said quickly, already pressing a fresh towel down over the worst of it. "Saw it. Found the path. I've got him."

Vek hissed through his teeth, body jolting under the pressure.

"I know," I whispered, sliding my hand into his again. "I know it hurts, baby. Stay with us."

His fingers curled weakly around mine. Sweat beaded along his temple. The rise of his chest had gone uneven, shallow and strained, but it kept rising. That was all I could ask for.

Riggs leaned back just enough to grab a bottle Mason handed over. "Gunner—hold the light right there. Liv—keep talking to him."

"Okay," I murmured, leaning closer to Vek's face. "It's just Riggs cleaning the wound. He's good, Vek. He's helped half the ridge and quite a few soldiers at one time or another. He's stubborn as hell, but he's good."

Another breath shuddered out of him, warm and damp against my cheek.

"You love me," he whispered, barely a thread of sound.

"Yes." My voice broke. "I love you. And I need you to breathe. That's all you focus on. Just breathe for me."

The bottle in Riggs's hand tilted and poured clean, cold saline across the wound. Blood and saline pooled in the towel beneath Vek's side and seeped warm against my knee. He jerked with the sting, muscles tightening hard enough that the floor creaked beneath us.

"Easy," Riggs murmured. "I know. I know. Almost done with the cleaning."

Gunner swallowed audibly, the sound tight and ragged. "How bad is it?"

Riggs didn't answer right away—never a good sign—but his hands didn't falter. He soaked another towel, pressed, tilted the light, and assessed again.

"It's a deep graze with a nasty exit," he finally said. "He lost a lot of blood, but the angle's in our favor. No lung. No gut."

Relief hit me so hard I gasped.

Vek's eyes fluttered. "Liv...?"

"I'm right here. You're safe," I whispered fiercely. "We've got you. You're going to be okay."

Riggs reached for the suture kit. "Keep holding his hand. This part's going to hurt."

My stomach flipped. "Riggs—*wait*—does he need something for pain?"

Riggs hesitated for only a breath—one heart-beat—before shaking his head. "I don't have anything strong enough to knock out a man his size. And we don't have time to sit on our hands waiting for an ambulance. We close it now, or he bleeds more than he can afford."

Vek drew in another uneven breath. "Liv... stay."

"I'm not going anywhere." I pressed my forehead to his. "You hold my hand as hard as you need to, do you hear me?"

With a subtle nod, his fingers tightened with surprising strength—desperation giving him one more push.

Riggs glanced at Gunner. "Hold the light steady. Mason—help me keep him from rolling if he reacts."

They shifted closer. The room felt too small, too warm, thick with fear and the metallic tang of blood.

Vek sucked in a sharp breath when the needle met his skin, every muscle in his chest going tight beneath Riggs' hands. His grip crushed my fingers, but I welcomed the pain—it meant he was still fighting, still here.

"I know," I whispered, brushing my thumb along the back of his knuckles. "I'm right here. You hold on to me."

Riggs worked in careful, steady pulls, his face tight with concentration. Mason braced a hand on Vek's shoulder in case he jerked. Gunner held the lamp so close I could feel the heat on my cheek.

No one spoke unless they had to. The whole world narrowed to Vek's ragged breathing and Riggs's steady hands.

Halfway through the stitches, Vek's eyes fluttered, losing their fight to stay open.

"Liv..." His voice cracked. "Tired."

My heart seized. "I know, baby. I know. Just a little longer." I leaned close, keeping his gaze pinned to mine. "Don't leave me yet. Stay with me."

He tried—*God*, he tried. His fingers tightened once more around mine, then loosened as another wave of pain rolled through him.

Riggs glanced up. "It's okay if he fades. I've got him. He's safe."

The words broke something loose in my chest, but I kept talking to Vek anyway, kept brushing his fur back, kept grounding him with every touch I could give.

When Riggs finally tied off the last stitch, he exhaled hard and sat back on his heels. "That's it," he said quietly. "Bleeding's stopped. He'll be weak as hell, but he's stable."

Stable.

The word hit so hard my breath stuttered. All the fear I'd been holding down punched its way to the surface.

I bent over Vek, forehead against his temple, tears soaking into his fur. "You hear that?" I whispered. "You're okay. You're safe. I've got you."

His breathing had gone heavy—slow, but steady. Each inhale rose beneath my palm in a soft, even rhythm.

Alive.

Covering the wound with a clean bandage, Riggs pressed down gently. "He'll rest now. Body's doing what it needs to do. If he needs blood, one of us can donate it, but I don't know how well it would mix with his own. For now, we will monitor him."

Gunner crouched on my other side, voice gentler than I'd expected from a man who'd had murder in his eyes minutes ago. "He's going to make it, Liv."

My throat closed. I nodded once, afraid the sound of my voice might crack too hard to recover from.

Vek's hand twitched weakly in mine. I held it tighter, bringing it to my cheek.

"I love you," I whispered against his skin. "I'm not leaving. Not for a second."

And finally—*finally*—some part of me allowed the truth to settle:

He wasn't slipping away. He was still here—still mine—his breath rising steady beneath my hands as the house settled quiet around us again.

CHAPTER 15

Home

Vek

A month had passed since the night she held me together on her living room floor. My body healed quickly, faster than Riggs had expected, but Liv still watched me closely, as if she expected a crack to split me open if she blinked too long.

This morning, her kitchen was warm with sunlight and the smell of cooking eggs. She stood at the stove with her hair twisted up, a curl slipping down the side of her neck. I loved when that curl fell loose. I didn't know why one small thing could matter so much, but it did.

June Bug darted around her ankles, tiny claws tapping on the tile. She bumped my foot as if she meant to challenge it, then puffed herself up, proud for no reason I could see. Boone sat beside my chair, giving me the look he only used when he'd decided he and I were choosing the same thing, no matter what Liv thought.

Liv turned, spatula in hand. When she saw me watching her, her smile spread slowly. "You're staring."

"I know," I said. My voice came out rough. I didn't mind.

She raised an eyebrow. "Something wrong?"

"No." I swallowed. "Something... right."

Her cheeks flushed, soft color rising under her skin. She set a plate in front of me, brushing her fingers across mine on purpose. That touch traveled down my spine. It had been a month without her body under mine, a month of her telling me to wait while I healed, and I had listened, but every part of me pulled toward her like it was instinct carved into bone.

I ate because she told me to. She sat across from me, our knees touching, and I had to steady my breath. When she shifted her chair closer, her sweet scent wrapped around me, and desire stirred sharp and sudden, like hunger I knew too well.

She took a sip of coffee like nothing had changed. "You're quiet this morning."

"I want you."

She froze. Heat rose fast across her face. "Vek…"

"You said to wait," I reminded her. "I waited."

Her breath caught. She set her coffee down, her hands unsteady. "You… you're healed enough?"

"Yes." I kept my voice low. "And I want you."

She looked at me as if the words touched her in places I couldn't see. Her eyes darkened. "Finish your breakfast," she whispered.

"No." I pushed the plate aside.

Shaking her head, her breathless laugh hit me like a warm hand on my chest. "You're serious."

"Yes." My chair creaked as I stood. She didn't resist when I pulled her up by the arm and kissed her, groaning at the taste of her mouth.

The kitchen faded as her hands slid up my chest, her body fitting against mine in a way I had memorized in too many nights of wanting. One warm breath from her brushed my jaw, and whatever restraint I had left went thin—ready to snap.

"Bedroom?" she asked, voice soft and thick with need.

She wasn't really asking.

"Now," I said.

She gasped when I lifted her, her legs locking around my hips, her arms around my neck. Her mouth found the side of my throat, soft first, then hungry, and the sound she made against my skin dragged a growl from deep inside me.

Heartbeats later, I pushed the bedroom door open with my shoulder. Her hips shifted, tightening her hold. Her whole body pressed against me—warm with want—and the last bit of patience I'd kept for a month snapped clean.

Her back met the bed, but she didn't let go—her fists curled in my shirt, dragging me down as if she needed me close. Her mouth captured mine, a kiss full of everything we'd both been starving for. Fire surged through me fast enough that I had to brace a hand beside her head to keep from giving her all my weight.

Her breath brushed my jaw. "I missed this."

She didn't need my answer. She felt it.

Hand sliding along her thigh, my fingers traced the inside where her skin grew hotter. She opened for me without hesitation, her hips rising to meet my hand. The sound she made hit deep in my chest, pulling a rough groan from me. Too long. Too many nights on the edge of wanting her while she told me to rest, heal, wait.

I had waited. Now my whole body ached for her.

She reached for me with urgency, pulling me closer, hands slipping into my fur. "I want you," she said again, voice trembling with need.

"I know," I murmured against her throat, kissing my way down the warm line of her skin.

Her laugh was breathless as she tugged my shirt up. I pulled it over my head, barely feeling the faint tug in my healing ribs. When my skin met hers, she arched, tracing the lines of muscle like she needed to feel all of me.

"God," she whispered, "you look good."

"You." I kissed her again, deeper. Her thighs tightened around my hips. My hand slipped beneath her shirt, her nipple hardening under my palm. She gasped and bit her lip, eyes heavy with desire.

"Take off," I said, ready to tear the fabric apart if I had to.

Panting hard, she lifted her arms. I pulled her shirt over her head, slow enough to feel her shiver under the drag of fabric. When I tossed it aside, she flushed, chest rising fast. I lowered my mouth to her breast, and her head fell back with a sharp breath.

"Vek—"

Her voice alone almost broke what control I had left.

I kissed her again, traced her with my hands and mouth—every sound she made pulled me deeper. When I reached the band of her pants, she lifted her hips to help. Her panties followed, and when she lay bare beneath me, my cock went so hard it hurt.

Her scent hit me hard, making my mouth water. My thumb brushed between her thighs, testing how ready she was, pleased when I found her drenched for me.

With a growl, I lowered myself between her thighs and tasted her for the first time since the night everything changed. Her cry shot through me like fire along the spine. She tried to cover her mouth, but I pulled her hand away and held it beside her hip.

"Let me hear you."

Her body trembled hard at the words, and she rolled toward my mouth, desperate for friction.

When I licked her again, focusing on the little bundle of nerves right above her entrance, she lost her breath entirely. Her thighs tightened around my head, not enough to stop me—enough to show me what she wanted. I slid my finger inside her and kept going until she was shaking, gasping, barely able to form my name.

"That—right there—God, don't stop—"

When her body tightened around my finger, I worked her harder, loving how she fell apart for me. She came hard, voice breaking into a sound that made every nerve in me stand on edge.

When she softened, I lifted my head. She lay panting, eyes dark, wanting me again.

"Come here," she whispered, reaching for me. "I want you inside me."

With my cock was already painfully hard, I slid up her body, kissing every place I'd tasted. She pushed my pants down with shaking hands. When her fingers wrapped around my cock, my thoughts scattered.

"Liv..."

Heat and slickness pulled me closer as she guided me between her thighs. I pressed forward—slow enough for her to take me, not slow enough to keep my control from breaking.

The first inch made her gasp. The second dug her nails into my shoulders. When I sank fully into her, she let out a sound I'd never forget—want, relief, something like love.

"Vek..." She cupped my face, pulling me down until our foreheads touched. "Don't hold back."

That was all I needed.

I thrust into her, slow at first, letting her body adjust. She met every stroke, hips rising, breath catching each time I went deeper. Tension coiled low in me, building fast

"More," she whispered.

I gave her more.

Her hands dragged down my back, her legs tightening around my hips. Her body clenched around me in pleasure, dragging me closer to the edge. When she whispered my name—voice cracking, full of wanting—I lost the last of my restraint.

When her release gripped her, she screamed my name, her body arching beneath mine. My name on her lips and the feel of her tightening around me dragged a groan from deep in my chest, and I followed, spilling into her with a force that shook my arms.

She held me through it—arms around my neck, legs locked around my hips, mouth against my cheek—while the world narrowed to heat and breath and her voice.

When the last tremor eased, she didn't let me move.

"Stay," she whispered against my skin.

Her breath warmed my throat. Her body softened beneath mine as the room grew quiet again. The house felt different—still, but not afraid. Outside, the ridge finally went still. Gunner had driven T-Bone off for good. No one was coming back up here looking for trouble. Not for her. Not for me.

Not anymore.

So I stayed. I always would.

THE END

Enjoyed Seduced by Sasquatch?

If <u>Seduced by Sasquatch</u> made you laugh, blush, or question your stance on large, hairy forest men, I would be *over the moon* if you left a review.

Your words help more readers find this wonderfully unhinged story, and they help indie authors like me keep creating chaotic, steamy, big-footed adventures in the woods.

If you'd like to share your thoughts (or confess that you now side-eye every tree line), you can leave a review here:

Amazon Review Link:
https://www.amazon.com/Seduced-Sasquatch-C-Varian-ebook/dp/B0FZ812P8B

Thank you from the bottom of my heart, and from the tall, mysterious, possibly-too-handsome creature lurking in the pines.

Your support means the world.

XOXO,

C.A. Varian

Acknowledgements

This book would not exist without those who carried me when I couldn't drag it out of the forest alone.

To my amazing Executive Assistant, Jessica—thank you for helping me keep my head on straight (even when I wandered off into the metaphorical woods). You make it possible for me to keep this wonderfully wild ride going.

To my incredible PA, Aly Dust—thank you for being a creative force, a hype queen, and a steady presence even when my brain was off wrestling imaginary Sasquatches.

To my super supportive Street Team—you are the echoing whoops in the trees. Your enthusiasm, love, and loyalty were the wind at my back...and occasionally the twig snapping behind me.

To my husband, children, and family—thank you for your patience, love, and for understanding that writing a book sometimes means disappearing into another world entirely.

To my cover designer, Leigh Cover Designs, ZONE ARTZ, and to the incomparable "Art Daddy" D'Arte Oriel—your talent brought this beast to life.

To my editor, Kate Seger—thank you for diving into this chaotic, big-footed adventure with a tight deadline, a tighter budget, and the patience of a saint. You got her done and then some.

To my readers—thank you for returning to the page, for believing in unlikely romances, questionable forest decisions, and the possibility that love might come with big footprints and an even bigger heart.

This book was a labor of love through one of the hardest years of my life. Battling neurological Lyme disease and tick-borne Bartonella made every day feel like trekking uphill in mud. Because of all of you, this book stomped out of the underbrush and onto the page.

From the bottom of my heart, thank you.
XOXO, Cherie

Also by C.A. Varian

Crown of the Phoenix Series
Crown of the Phoenix

Crown of the Exiled

Crown of the Prophecy

Mate of the Phoenix

Shadowed by Prophecy

Shadowed by the Veil (Coming Soon)

My Alien Mate Series
My Alien Protector

My Alien Rescuer (coming soon!)

Other World Series
The Other World

The Other Key

The Other Fate

Hazel Watson Mystery Series
Kindred Spirits: Prequel

The Sapphire Necklace
Justice for the Slain
Whispers from the Swamp
Crossroads of Darkness
The Spirit Collector
The Darkness that Follows (Coming Soon)

The Cursed Waters Duet
Song of Death
Goddess of Death

Survivor & Savior Duet
Saving Scarlett
Keeping Caroline

Standalones

Second Chance with Santa
When Everly Saved Emerald Hollow
Spirit of the Dying Flower
Seduced by Sasquatch
The Moon-Cursed Crown (Coming March 2026)
The Gladiatrix & the Fallen Son (Coming Soon)
Wings of the Forgotten (Coming Soon with J. Paige)

About C.A. Varian

Born and raised in the heart of Louisiana's Cajun Country, I'm a passionate writer of dark, fantasy, paranormal, and even alien romances—if there's a romance involved, chances are I've written it. My stories are filled with mystery, magic, and intense emotional connections that keep readers on the edge of their seats.

When I'm not writing, you'll find me creating special editions of my books packed with all the bells and whistles—character art, exclusive swag, and more for my readers to treasure. I love connecting with fans, whether it's through my TikTok shop, my website, or in person at events where I can share the stories I pour my heart into.

A proud mother and new grandmother, I've faced many challenges in life, including a battle with neurological Bartonella and Lyme disease, but I've never let it define me. Writing is my escape and my passion, and with the support of my amazing assistant Jessica, my husband Trevor, and my daughters, Arianna and Brianna, I'm living my dream of writing full-time. Even my two youngest sisters pitch in, helping me with various tasks for the business—it's truly a family affair!

At home in the coastal region of Mississippi, surrounded by love, laughter, and inspiration, I'm never without my two Shih Tzus, Charlie and Luna, along with my three mischievous cats—Ramses, Simba, and Cookie. (We just lost Simba and I cannot bear to remove his name yet). Whether I'm doting on my furry companions, reading, or soaking up family time, every moment is a precious one.

Join me as I continue to create worlds full of romance, adventure, and unforgettable characters that you won't want to put down!